PRAISE FOR *COUNTRY OF THE BIRCH TREES*

"Kristin McGlothlin does that miraculous thing: she imagines a world and peoples it with convincing characters."

—Rodman Philbrick, Newbery Honor–winning novelist

"The author deftly handles complex issues, like cultural background and mental health, in a gentle but realistic manner."

—*Kirkus Reviews*

"*Country of the Birch Trees* is a moving tribute to the trials and tribulations of a thirteen-year-old in a small town who merely wants the best for those around her."

—BookLife Reviews

"McGlothlin's story shows how three thirteen-year-olds approach family issues with sincerity and kindness."

—Adrian Fogelin, award-winning author of the Neighborhood Novels series

"Curiosity, compassion, and creativity abound as three best friends turn their detective work from casual whimsy to an authentic exploration of art, human behavior, and Native American culture."

—Susan Koehler, author of *Dahlia in Bloom* and *Nobody Kills Uncle Buster and Gets Away with It*

COUNTRY OF THE BIRCH TREES

COUNTRY OF THE BIRCH TREES

SOURLAND MOUNTAIN SERIES BOOK 3

KRISTIN McGLOTHLIN

Sourland Mountain
•BOOKS•

This is a work of fiction. Names, characters, organizations, places, events, and incidents are either products of the author's imagination or are used fictitiously.

Published by Sourland Mountain Books, Jupiter
sourlandmountainbooks.com

GIRL FRIDAY PRODUCTIONS

Edited and designed by Girl Friday Productions
www.girlfridayproductions.com

Cover design: Paul Barrett
Project management: Reshma Kooner and Laura Dailey
Cover illustration: Kristina Swarner

ISBN (paperback): 978-1-7332865-2-7

First edition

To Mom and Dad

There was a child went forth every day,
And the first object he looked upon and
received with wonder or pity or love or
dread, that object he became,
And that object became part of him for the day
or a certain part of the day . . .

—*Leaves of Grass* by Walt Whitman

Sourland Mountain is in central New Jersey, twenty minutes from the town of Princeton. On top of the mountain sit two neighborhoods. The first neighborhood has similar style homes with well-kept lawns and paved streets. They have plenty of land around them and are buffered by woods. North of it is the Backwoods of Sourland Mountain. The houses there are eclectic and not all of the roads are paved. The homes in this neighborhood back up to the park and wildlife sanctuary named the Sourland Mountain Preserve.

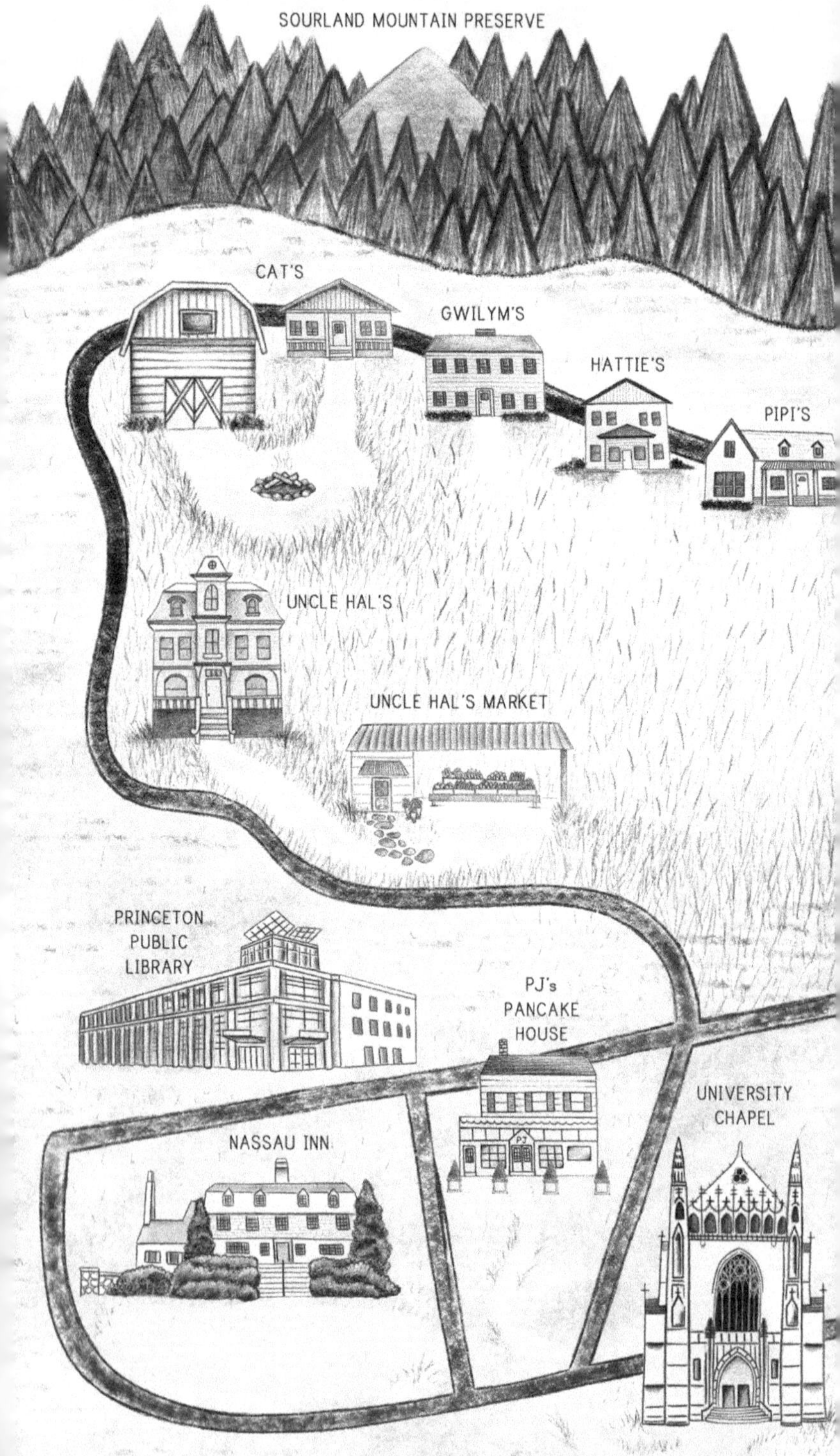
SOURLAND MOUNTAIN PRESERVE
CAT'S
GWILYM'S
HATTIE'S
PIPI'S
UNCLE HAL'S
UNCLE HAL'S MARKET
PRINCETON
PUBLIC
LIBRARY
PJ's
PANCAKE
HOUSE
UNIVERSITY
CHAPEL
NASSAU INN

JOE'S
LIBRARY
LIBRARY
LAKE SATURDAY
GEORGE'S
RIVER'S
OLD BARN
PARTY
TOOLS
MOVIE
MUSIC
TIGER'S TALE
WREN'S GARAGE
ART
Kristin Heron

SEPTEMBER 1978

"Ouch!" River Wren was leaning against a tree, rubbing her scratched ankle. Assisted by the cold fall wind, the tree rustled. "It's okay," River reassured it. It shook its branches again. "Don't worry, the branch barely got me." The wind blew a handful of multicolored leaves at her like fingers. "It's okay!" River repeated. "See?" She showed her wound. "It'll heal just fine." She pushed herself from the trunk and began walking again.

River's damp black hair clung to her chestnut-colored skin at the back of her neck. She squinted at the blank sky. Her saddle shoes and the bottom of her blue-and-red plaid wool pants were splashed with mud. She didn't like trekking through the woods if she didn't have to. *Why are we walking to the library anyway, when we could have driven?*

A few feet in front of River was her best friend, George Janson. George was yelling at her mom. "Mom, wait up!" she said again as she stepped on a pile of wet leaves covered in mud that squirted onto her sneakers. River watched George's sand-colored mane swing downward as she examined the damage to her shoes.

In front of the two girls was George's mom. River studied the back of Mrs. Janson's coat. It looked expensive, like the rest of her clothes. Her periwinkle dress peeked out from under the wool coat, which was a deeper shade of periwinkle. Her hair, the same color as George's, was rolled into a big swirl. The three continued to walk through the woods.

"This is an adventure!" Mrs. Janson said, swinging her arms like a windup toy.

"George," River whispered. "George."

"What?"

"Why are we walking to the library in this weather? I'm cold and sweaty."

"I don't know why. Thought she'd want to drive her new car. But this morning she was all in a tizzy about the idea of walking through the forest to the library." George maneuvered around a tree branch.

A bird called. River looked up to see if she could spot it. "Your mom's going to ruin her pretty clothes," she said as she continued to scan the tree branches. Unable to find the chirper, River turned her gaze to Mrs. Janson's large black leather purse—coordinated to her outfit—then to the black rubber work boots she was wearing. Boots that somehow had only the tiniest amount of mud on them. River smirked. *Too bad she didn't tell George we should wear boots too.*

River grumbled, stomping one foot after the other onto the soggy ground. She usually didn't feel so grumpy, but she hadn't expected to be trudging through the wet leaves and mud to get to the library today. If River's mom would've suggested this journey, it would've been an adventure, and they would've been fully prepared in their warm hats, scarves, coats, mittens, and boots. Unlike Mrs. Wren, Mrs. Janson looked out of her element in the woods. River agreed with her younger sister, Savannah, that Mrs. Janson looked like Princess Grace, the American actress who became a princess, with every inch of her the height of elegance.

With the image of Grace Kelly still in her mind, River followed the other two inside the library and into the bright entrance. She elbowed George. "We should go to the restroom first to get this mud off."

George nodded. They turned left into a narrow, dimly lit hallway, past a bulletin board filled with different colored papers, and into the pink-tiled ladies' room.

"Geez, it's cold in here," River said as she grabbed paper towels from the dispenser, dabbed them lightly with water, and began rubbing the bottom of her pant leg.

"You're awfully moody this morning," commented George, working on her shoe.

"I know." River started on her other pant leg. "I just wasn't prepared for—"

"A fun adventure to the library!" George stood up and dropped the used paper towel in the wastebasket.

Mrs. Janson was waiting for them. She had changed into navy heels, and now magically another even larger bag appeared on her arm, apparently containing her boots and her purse. "I'm going over to the cookbook section. You two come and get me when you're done finding your books."

River felt the librarians watching her as she and George walked to the children's books section. She took a couple of steps, then looked back to make sure she wasn't leaving dirt marks. *All clean.* They stopped in front of the Nancy Drew section, like they did every trip to the library.

Ever since they were little, River, George, and their friend Joe had been in competitions usually invented and run by Joe. Sometimes he competed against the two girls; sometimes it was everyone for themselves. This one was the girls against the boy. For the current competition, Joe had challenged them to see who could finish reading their favorite series: for Joe, the Hardy Boys series; for River and George, the Nancy Drew series.

"What number are we on?" asked River, running her eyes across the row of Nancy Drew books. They glowed against the faux-wood bookcase. She thought the color of the spines looked like lemon rinds faded by the sun, if they could fade in the sun.

"Thirty-four, *The Hidden Window Mystery,*" said George, handing it to River.

River looked at the cover. Nancy stood in a red bathrobe shining a flashlight on a peacock with a gigantic tail. River frowned. *Not a very exciting cover picture.* She opened the book to a black-and-white illustration of Nancy and her best friend, George, falling through a trapdoor. *Now that's more exciting.*

River commented to George, "You know Joe likes to keep us busy." She handed the book back to George.

"Yeah," George said, turning to the back cover.

"We're always in some kind of competition. Remember when we were little, it was who could run fastest from the front door of my house down the hill to the lake, then it was eating contests, and now it's reading contests." River grinned, thinking of all the years they'd been competing.

George shook her head. "It's a boy thing."

River asked, "Do you know what number of the Hardy Boys books Joe's on?"

"I'm on thirty-seven," Joe Farrington announced.

"Geez, Joe. I didn't hear you come up." River looked at Joe with his ruffled light-brown hair and wire-framed glasses.

Ignoring her comment, Joe held up a book. "Look what I found. An old series called The Three Investigators. I was putting them on the shelf earlier. They look good. Don't know if they'll be as good as the Hardy Boys." He looked at his watch. "Oh! My break's over. Gotta get back to shelving books. See ya!"

As Joe walked away, River noticed two paperbacks he had in addition to The Three Investigators and Hardy Boys books. She smiled. "Joe's got two more Elmore Leonard novels. I guess his mom hasn't caught him reading them yet." The two girls started walking toward the front of the library to the checkout desk.

"Joe thinks he's an adult," said George. "How long's he been volunteering at the library?" They had reached the librarian. George placed her books on the desk.

"Since last summer," River told her.

"Why does he want to volunteer here?" asked George.

"He loves reading, so I guess it's the place he'd want to be," said River.

"Still, it's weird," continued George. "A thirteen-year-old volunteering." Their books were checked out and they were making their way to the front door.

Mrs. Janson had her checked-out cookbooks under her arm and was waiting for the girls. She'd changed back into the boots. "All set, girls? Ready to make our journey home?" Mrs. Janson said, looking jubilant.

George sighed. "Mom, can we walk back along the road instead? River and I don't really want to walk through the woods again."

Mrs. Janson's excited expression fell from her face. "Well, I guess, if you girls would prefer," she muttered. They stepped outside to a cloudy sky and began their walk home along the roadside. River, George, and Joe lived with their families on Lake Saturday. River's house was next door to George's and Joe's was across the lake from them. They'd lived in their houses since they were infants.

River's heart beat faster. She looked at George, who was staring at the sidewalk. *Did we do something wrong?* As if hearing her friend's thoughts, George slumped her shoulders.

"Come on," said Mrs. Janson. Every step she took seemed to be drudgery.

She set the solemn mood for the rest of the way. River didn't say a word; George continued staring down. When they reached the Janson household, Mrs. Janson said to River, "Have a good rest of the day, River." She didn't sound like she meant it. *George's mom is overreacting, right? How did we spoil her day?*

River's mom was in her studio-shed working, the radio playing soft rock. In her bedroom, River arranged the library books on her bookshelf in the order that she would read them. Her heartbeat had returned to normal. She heard her dad's voice say, "Going to the Party Store. Anyone coming?"

"Going to the Party Store, River?" Savannah asked as she danced in their bedroom doorway. Sunlight flashed through her red hair as she wiggled.

"Yes," River said in relief. *Something I really would like to do!*

The sisters sat in the front seat of the truck next to their dad on the ride to the store. His window was cracked open a little so that River felt the cool wind on her face and neck, but the rest of her was cozy with the warm air from the vents. They rode without the radio on. When Mr. Wren was driving, he didn't want to listen to music. He'd told them long ago that when he was driving, he was coming up with music for his band. Heavy metal music. Their dad was the lead vocalist and guitarist of Beowulf's Brother. The other band members were George's dad on drums and Joe's dad on bass. They played gigs around Rocky Hill and Princeton, and they were expanding beyond those areas. Until Beowulf's Brother became a huge moneymaker, Mr. Wren would remain a full-time mechanic at his car repair shop, Wren's Garage; George's dad would still be a carpenter (the band practiced in the Janson garage); and Joe's dad, the owner of the local hardware store.

The first landmark on the trip to the Party Store was the old barn. When River and her friends walked to the Party Store, they did not go inside the barn. Half of its roof had collapsed, and many of the boards holding the structure up had fallen down. Savannah began giggling beside River. "Oh, it's coming up!" As their car moved past the old barn Savannah squealed, "Fairies must live in there!"

"We've never seen fairies anywhere near it when we've walked past it on the way to the Party Store," River reminded her.

"I have," Savannah said in a low voice. "In the windows."

"You never told me that," said River, grinning at her little sister.

"They only let some people see them. They don't want people invading their space."

"And they let you see them?"

"Yes, they do," said Savannah, sitting up straight.

The Jewett farmstead was up next. Aggie Jewett was River's age, and her brother, Hal, and Savannah were four years younger. As the car went by, River thought of the inside of the Jewetts' bright red barn and of the mural there that had been painted by their great-great-great-grandma Jewett in the 1850s. Aggie had told River the painting was in the style of the famous American artist Grandma Moses, even though Moses's artwork came much, much later. River had seen the wall painting many times. The picture showed a light blue sky with clouds and distant mountains, then houses and a field, and horses and horse-drawn carriages, and people . . . At the bottom of the picture was the Jewetts' farm. There were cows in the field now. When Hal grew up, he'd told them many times, he wanted to have a big garden and a market there next to the animals.

At the bottom of the hill a road led one way to the history-filled town of Princeton and the university, or the other way to Rocky Hill, a place of equal historical importance. It was not too long ago that River had walked Nassau Street and Palmer Square. The horseshoe-shaped square stopped at the entrance to Princeton University. George's mom was a secretary in one of the buildings on campus. *Maybe Joe will work in the university library when he grows up.* The majority of people she observed on Nassau Street weren't dressed in fancy clothes. They didn't act snobby. This was an academic town. In Princeton, people were more interested in ideas than in looking good. There were rich people in the town of Princeton, however, and some did dress like Mrs. Janson. Many times River and her family had driven past the large houses of the wealthy people. She felt she wouldn't be comfortable living in one of them. Too much space. She didn't need that many rooms to have to take care of.

Her dad saw Princeton only as a place with either stuffy know-it-alls or rich people. "And neither," he'd told the girls numerous times, "know the first thing about fixing their cars, which is good for my business." He pulled into a parking spot in front of the Party Store.

River and Savannah were out of the car and into the store before he'd shut his door. The row of stores resembled a shoebox, an old one with worn corners. The Party Store was the first one on the left. Joe's dad's hardware store, the movie theater, and the music store were next down the line. The hardware store was cozy and smelled of cedar. River thought the movie theater must be one of the smallest anywhere. It showed one movie at a time. The floor smelled musty with a hint of soda. She preferred the metallic instrument smells in the music store owned by Marley Jones. He would be standing at the counter concentrating on papers in front of him when River and her dad came into the store. Marley would look up, welcome them, then return his attention to whatever he was looking at. Her dad purchased everything for the band there. Joe's mom's art gallery was farther down the road from the shops. She'd had the gallery for a couple of years. She showcased artists from around the tristate area of New York, New Jersey, and Connecticut.

In the Party Store, River and Savannah stopped at the front counter where the candy was while their dad headed to the liquor section. As was routine, after their purchases they would meet in the grocery area.

"Where are the Gobstoppers?" Savannah's hand fluttered over each section of candy. She stared at an older kid behind the counter. "Don't you have Gobstoppers?" He pointed to them. "Oh, thank goodness!" she said. "I'm getting those, a Heath bar, and a box of candy cigarettes," she yelled at River, who was standing next to her.

River had selected rock candy, a Hershey's bar, and bubble gum. Her parents allowed them to choose three types of candy. She decided on five gumballs in each color available, reasoning that she was still getting just one type of candy. The girls laid their finds on the counter in front of the cashier. River opened her change purse and waited for the total. She paid for the candy and took the two brown paper bags from him.

They traveled back to the grocery area, where their dad was standing by the produce with a shopping cart. "What's on your mom's list?" The three went through Mrs. Wren's list, crossing off their finds. They did this as fast as they could, since it was the boring part of shopping.

On the ride home River and Savannah swayed back and forth with the curves in the road; Mr. Wren focused on the scene in front of them while working on a song in his head.

After helping put the groceries away, River decided to go to George's house. Inside she smelled cherry pie. Mrs. Janson *did* make the best cherry pies. River was curious about what kind of mood George's mom would be in. River was highly sensitive to other people's emotions and feelings. A person's high spirits raced through her body like a speedboat flying across the surface of the lake, and someone's gloomy demeanor sunk her to the bottom of the lake.

River sat down in a kitchen chair next to George. River accepted a piece of pie from Mrs. Janson and took her first bite. "The crust is just the right crustiness to complement the tart-sweetness of the cherries," she said. George agreed.

"I'm glad you like it, River," Mrs. Janson said, her face bright with enthusiasm. "It's always a big seller at the market." She paused in front of the oven. "Maybe Mrs. Farrington would be interested in serving them at her gallery openings." She lowered the oven door and pulled out another pie with a perfect lattice design on top. "And your mom should have her pottery sold there too," said George's mom to River. "Your mom is a fine artist."

River agreed. "What she loves best is making mugs and bowls on her potter's wheel. And she doesn't get upset when they break in the kiln." She wondered if Mrs. Janson got upset if a latticed top on one of her pies came out broken.

"Well," said Mrs. Janson. "I don't always enjoy making pies. Especially when they don't come out right when they need to be perfect."

"They don't have to be per—" George grabbed River's arm before she could finish the word. "I mean, they always look perfect to me, Mrs. Janson."

Mrs. Janson smiled. "Thank you, River. That's kind of you to say."

"We're going to go hang out in my room. Pie was scrumptious as always, Mom."

The girls put their dishes and forks in the sink and headed for George's bedroom. They each selected an area to sit around a collection of comic books. Comic books were their other favorite reads along with the Nancy Drew books. River paused from opening her *Casper the Friendly Ghost* issue and listened to the sound of a creaking of cupboard door being opened in the kitchen, followed by a *pop, pop, pop* that made her put down the book. It sounded like plastic hitting wood. She glanced at George, who looked frozen. Then at the same time, they got up and rushed into the kitchen to see George's mom throwing Tupperware at an open cupboard. Each piece she launched missed the opening, making her throw the next one harder. The noise rattled River's ears. George screamed, "For Pete's sake, Mom, stop it! Stop throwing the containers!"

"I hate them! They keep falling out!" Mrs. Janson's face was the color of cherries, her eyes shining like two blue buttons.

With her heart pumping violently, River helped George gather the plasticware and put it inside the cupboard. Meanwhile, Mrs. Janson sat in a chair at the table and put her head in her hands. After the girls finished, they went back to George's bedroom.

Sitting on the shag carpet, River worried her heart wouldn't slow down. She and George had returned to reading their comic books. River's mind couldn't focus on the cute ghost on the pages. She wasn't sure if she should keep quiet about what she'd just witnessed. *Should I say something about what just happened in the kitchen?*

George was braiding a small section of her hair, yanking the pieces together.

"George?" River reached for her friend's hand.

"Why don't you go home?" George said, frowning at her braid.

"Are you sure?" River asked.

"Go!" Tears began rolling down George's face.

River got up. "Okay, see you later."

The cool air patted her cheeks on the way home. She kept her tears from flowing until she was in her bed with the covers over her and the door closed. Her cat, High-Five, snuggled with her. She stroked his back. His fur was white except for the top of his head and his ears, which were black. At this moment she really appreciated that he was a cuddler.

Securing the animal under her arm, she let her tears soak her pillow. Savannah was playing in the living room and her sister's voice soothed her. It sounded like a recording of a child singing "diddle-diddle-diddle" and "doe-doe-doe." River turned onto her back, releasing High-Five, who moved to the end of her bed, and closed her eyes. She fell asleep. When she awoke it was dark in her room. She sat up. *What time is it? Did I sleep through dinner?*

Her family was at the kitchen table eating dinner.

"Well, there's the sleeping bear. You didn't budge when I looked in on you," said her mom. "Are you feeling okay, River?"

She slunk into her chair. "Yes. Just tired."

"You look pale," said her mom. "Here, eat." She passed River a bowl of potato salad. "And there're pork chops. Savannah, please pass the plate to your sister."

River relaxed as she ate and listened to her dad describe a Porsche that'd been dropped off at the shop. He was glad he was getting regular business, because the owner was raising the rent again. Her mom talked about being pleased with the mugs she'd pulled out of the kiln. Savannah hummed while stuffing food into her mouth.

❧

The next day River walked under the banner that read "10th Annual Sourland Mountain Market Day" with Savannah charging after her. River looked forward to the event on the Jewetts' farm. She looked forward to the smell of the apple cider and the music of local bands—Beowulf's Brother had performed at the first Market Day—playing on the stage. As River walked to her mom's table with a box filled with ceramic mugs and bowls, she passed other participants setting up their tables. Everyone involved expected a good turnout, as the event had gained popularity each year. The day's crisp breeze accentuated the patter of the merchants and musicians setting up.

The sisters had been dropped off by their dad on his way to the repair shop; their mom had arrived earlier to set up the table. Walking toward them was Aggie. “Hi, River. Hi, Savannah,” she said. River glanced behind Aggie to up near the barn where the Jewetts’ cows were mooing. “What’s it like constantly hearing cows outside your window?” she asked. Sometimes River could hear them from her house.

“Oh, it’s alright. They’re friendly and have different personalities. They’re smelling all the food and want to know what’s going on.”

“Do you want to go to Mrs. Janson’s table to see if we can get an early sample?” Aggie asked River. The wind swept Aggie’s brown bangs. She was holding one of her two braids.

“Let’s go!” She thought her own words sounded fake, and they hurt her stomach.

George was smoothing out the tablecloth while her mom was at the back of their car arranging her pies. George looked up as they approached and locked eyes with River. *Is she sending me a message that it’s a good day or a bad day so far for her mom?*

“Hi!” said Aggie. “Any chance there’s a small sample we could taste? So, you know, we can spread the word how amazing your pies are?”

River braced herself, waiting for Mrs. Janson to turn around.

"Yes," she answered in a friendly tone. "I have a cherry pie with latticework that fell apart during baking. Would you like a slice?"

River put her hand to her mouth as she giggled. Mrs. Janson looked like Mrs. Jetson from Savannah's favorite Saturday morning cartoon. Her hair was curled under then combed and hairsprayed so that there were two edges that jutted out from each ear. River was amazed at how hair spray could make ladies' hairdos appear space-age by defying gravity.

"Yes, please," said Aggie.

"River?" Mrs. Janson asked. River nodded, pressing her lips together to hold back the giggle. She looked at the segmented strips of crisscrossed baked dough on top of the pie. It looked scrumptious even with the imperfection. "Yes, please."

"Yes?" asked Mrs. Janson.

"She said yes," George said, as she laid out two paper plates with plastic forks.

Aggie was still smiling. Lucky for her, she only knew *this* Mrs. Janson.

After Aggie and River finished their pieces of pie, they said "So long" and each went to her own mom's table. Aggie's mom sold cheese they made from the milk of their cows. River loved all their cheeses. Her family kept the refrigerator stocked with Jewett Farm cheese. River saw Hal Jewett at his family's table. He was seated with crutches beside him. Hal had fallen out of a tree and broken his leg. He waved at her and she reciprocated.

As the day progressed, River helped with customers and took breaks to walk around and see the other crafts. Mrs. Wren had brought River to the event since she was three years old. By now she recognized most of the merchants and nodded or waved at them. She stopped at Joe's mom's table, filled with artwork from her gallery. There were wood boxes that Mr. Janson had made for her to fill with original acrylic and oil paintings done by local artists, and on a folding divider were hung large paintings. Mrs. Farrington was trying to persuade River's mom to sell her mugs at the gallery, but Mrs. Wren thought her ceramics weren't that high quality—which was nonsense. She always said, "My pieces are more for craft shows." River noticed an invitation lying on the table. It was for an opening at the gallery on the first Friday of November. The image on it was a portrait of a Native American with text that said, "Nanticoke Lenni-Lenape Tribesman." River put the invitation in her back pocket and continued on her way around the market. Every so often her mind would return to the portrait on the card.

Mr. Wren's side of the family was from the local Lenni-Lenape tribe. He had never talked to her and her sister about the Lenape culture; River guessed he didn't know much about it. His parents had died when he was around her age, and he had an older brother in Idaho whom he didn't speak to. River and Savannah hadn't seen their uncle in years.

However, River had become interested in this side of herself. She'd become more aware of her and her dad's physical features, comparing her appearance with how the people in her neighborhood looked. Unlike most of those she'd grown up with, she and her dad had black hair, dark eyes, and skin the color that George said was like her mom's cinnamon dough. The other side of River's heritage, her mom's side, was Irish. Her mom's and

Savannah's hair was reddish-brown, their skin burned easily, and their eyes were greenish blue.

River glanced at the vendors' faces, on the lookout for ones with features like hers and her dad's. Instead, they had white complexions like her mom and sister. This hadn't bothered her until recently. She'd accepted since she was little that the characters in her picture books looked like her mom and sister, and Nancy Drew had light skin, too, and was described as sometimes having blonde hair and sometimes reddish-blonde hair. She didn't like Nancy Drew any more or less because of what she looked like. But she was not a real person. *Where are the people who look like me?*

She'd had lessons in school on Native American history. Maybe the Lenape tribe had been mentioned once, twice? She wasn't positive. She had learned that all of the Native American tribes made arts and crafts. But what else was special and unique about her culture? She hadn't asked her mom or dad. Her many thoughts about the Lenape tribe swirled around in her head now.

The next morning was Sunday. When River woke up, she jumped out of bed, paused at the closed bedroom door, and listened. *Did I beat him to the porch this morning?* River believed she could tell by the silence in the house whether her dad was up. The air inside the house would tell her. She imagined that invisible curtains dropped down from the ceilings inside her house at night. In the morning, if her dad came out of his and her mom's bedroom first, he would disturb these curtains and send ripples through the air that River could feel. By the time all five of the family members, which included High-Five, were up and walking around, the curtains had disintegrated into the finest tissue paper and then completely dissolved, to reappear that night after they'd all gone to bed. And even though High-Five moved around the house at night, he didn't have enough weight to move the invisible curtains.

This was a part of her Sunday routine: to wake up before her dad and, depending on the season, beat him to the deck or to the enclosed porch. It was fall, so they would be in the porch. *Darn!* She sighed and walked into the room. "You got here first!"

He was sitting in one of the two swinging metal chairs, which were painted white and had bright lemon-colored cushions. His arms were resting on the chair arms and one hand held a ceramic mug of steaming coffee. She knew he'd been gazing out at the sun teasing the lake's surface with its first rays of light. "I didn't know it was a competition," he said.

"You know it is," River corrected him, as she sat in the metal swing chair next to him. Not turning his head from the window, he smiled.

"How was the market yesterday? I had too much to do at the shop to get over." He looked down at his oil- and dirt-stained hands and moved his fingers like he was playing his guitar. "Gonna have to work on that song today." Then looking at her, he asked, "Did your mom sell much?"

"About five or six mugs and a couple of tea bowls," said River. She wanted to give her dad higher numbers. She wanted him to be impressed with the sales of her mom's clay pieces. But she didn't sell that much in general.

"Maybe she should try making something else," her dad suggested. "Like," he scratched his unshaven chin, "what else could she make?"

High-Five swerved his body around River's legs. She picked him up and put him on her lap. "She could make pictures using clay."

"Pictures using clay." Her dad said each word with a nod in between.

She knew he had no clue what that meant. "I saw them yesterday. A lady had a piece of wood that was varnished. Then she'd made apples out of clay and glued them on it. She painted the apples too."

He took another sip of coffee. "These are handy mugs your mom makes. No doubt about that. I just wish she sold more of them." He emphasized what he said with his mug. "This is useful."

River stared at the glistening sunlight riding on the lake. Then she thought of the idea she'd had when she'd looked at the other tables yesterday. "There should be a table with Lenape arts and crafts." Her stomach tightened. She didn't know how her dad would react to this suggestion.

"Lenape crafts, huh?" His eyes were focused out on the lake. "Where'd you get that idea?"

"I just noticed that there aren't any things like that at yesterday's show or any show Mom and Savannah and I go to."

"Well, there's a reason for that." He sat up in his chair, making it squeak. "No one wants to buy that stuff."

"What stuff? I don't know what *that stuff* looks like. I mean, I'm half Lenape and I've never seen any Lenape art. And I know all tribes have their own kind of art."

"How do you know that?" His voice rose, then fell into a softer volume. "People around here don't want to buy those things."

"But you don't even know what *those things* are, Dad, and neither do I." High-Five dropped off her lap and trotted into the kitchen.

"Do your teachers teach you about the Lenape tribe?"

"I was trying to remember if they did. They may have mentioned our name."

River's dad looked at her. "Our name?" His expression went from questioning to concerned. "I haven't shared much with you about your heritage. I haven't taught you—or your sister—about our culture, have I? Or even your mom."

River shrugged. "That's okay."

In that moment before he had included Savannah and her mom, there had been a warmth in River's chest. She liked when her dad thought of the two of them as separate from her mom and sister. When the four of them stood together, she and her dad looked like father and daughter and her mom and Savannah looked like mother and daughter. There was something about looking alike on the outside that made you feel closer to that person on the inside.

They remained silent for a while, like they often did in this time together.

River heard High-Five meow in the kitchen. His food bowl was empty. "Just wait," she called to him. He gave a low meow that meant he couldn't. Her dad was sipping his coffee. He was growing a beard or else just hadn't shaved in a while; she didn't know which. He worked hard as a mechanic and she'd heard that he was good at it. When she'd been in his shop with him she saw that he liked repairing cars. Wren's Garage was an organized operation. Her dad did everything from fixing the cars to answering the telephone. He had two mechanics who worked in the shop with him. One of the employees had a son named Ralph Edwards. Ralph was in the same grade as River, George, and Joe. He was mainly Joe's friend. He was quiet and didn't say much around her and George. Joe told River that Ralph liked taking long walks in the woods. He'd stay there until sunset. When she asked what he did in there, Joe said he carried a notebook with him. "Maybe he writes stories?" Joe suggested.

Stories. There must be a lot of stories about and by the Lenape people. Maybe she would see if the library had any books on them, or if there were any mentions of them in books on New Jersey or Delaware. She'd have to do some investigating.

River heard a door open. *Darn.* Someone else was up. She heard her mom chatting with High-Five while Meow Mix was being poured into his bowl. A moment later her mom stepped out into the porch with her cup of coffee. "Good morning, my sweets." She leaned over and kissed her husband on the cheek. He smiled and maybe even blushed a little. She glided her hand over River's hair as she moved to the couch. "Did you sleep well?" River said she had.

"Looks like a beautiful morning. I'm glad the girls and I got everything back here yesterday from the Jewetts so we don't have to go back today."

"I said I'd go back and load up anything you couldn't," her dad said.

"I know, dear. I know you don't mind going back but I didn't bring as much." She smoothed the front of her robe. "It wasn't as crowded this year. I'm not sure why. Maybe they didn't get the word out early enough." She sipped her coffee. "Oh well."

Mr. Wren frowned at his coffee mug.

The TV started making noises. Savannah was looking for a cartoon show to watch. "There's nothing on Sunday," River had told her again and again, but her sister wouldn't listen to her. She counted *one-two-three-four* and heard the dial click that meant Savannah had turned off the TV.

The Sunday morning father-daughter time was officially over when Savannah flounced into the room. She went over and flopped on top of her mom. "There's nothing on TV," she complained.

"I tell you every . . ." River started to repeat herself when Savannah stuck out her tongue.

"I'm going outside to see my fishies." Savannah slid off her mom, grabbed her coat by the door, and headed down to the dock. River decided to follow her.

She closed the screen door behind her and walked across the deck to the wood stairs. She put her hand on the railing, which was made of birch branches. At the bottom of the seventeen steps, she plopped her feet on the sand and walked toward the dock, past the rocks that formed the firepit, and hopped onto the metal dock, making it bounce. Savannah had her legs crossed and was looking down at the sparkling water. River sat beside her sister.

"See my fishies?" Savannah pointed at the tiny fish swimming around in the glowing water. River loved the color the sun made the water in the morning. It looked like little gemlike fish floating on gold silk fabric in a shoebox diorama. Savannah just needed to check on her fish, because she didn't sit long. River watched her sister run off the dock to find her next thing to do.

River looked up at the house. When you lived on a lake, the front of the house faced the lake, and the side facing the road was the back of the house. Their house was on top of a hill. On the left were the stairs that led onto the sand. The last step was parallel to a rock wall. In front of it was the firepit. On either side of the beach were birch trees.

Savannah was crouched in a little stand of the trees, digging with her hands in the dirt. She liked getting dirty; she would have liked walking to the library with Mrs. Janson. She and River were still in their pj's. Their mom was used to washing the sand marks out of Savannah's pj's. River thought her sister shouldn't be allowed to play in her pajamas. That's not what they were for. She stood up and started walking toward her sister. "Savannah, come on. Let's go up and get our clothes on, and you can come back down and play."

"I found rocks buried here!" She held one in each hand. River looked at the flat, oval gray rocks. They were larger than her sister's hands. "I'm going to bury them. Then figure out something to do with them. Don't tell *anyone* they're here."

"Yeah, sure. Come on. Let's change clothes." As they reached the deck, River heard footsteps and looked over to see Mrs. Janson heading toward them carrying what looked like two pie pans covered with dish towels.

"What were you burying, Savannah?" asked Mrs. Janson.

Savannah smiled at Mrs. Janson, her idol, and said, "Oh, I can't tell you! I would if I could!" River laughed.

"Oh, okay." George's mom glanced at River, who shrugged. "I brought two pies for you, blueberry and cherry. George is up and dressed if you want to come over." River took the pies and said she'd be over. Mrs. Janson was acting normal, like other moms River knew. Her shoulders relaxed. Maybe George's mom was happier on the weekends?

NOVEMBER

It was the beginning of the month on a Wednesday after school, and River was sitting on top of the dock, which was stacked in three sections on the beach. She was wearing her yellow windbreaker and her white sneakers. Every year at this time the dock was taken out of the water and stored on the beach by her dad, George's dad, and Joe's dad—in other words, by Beowulf's Brother. River's dad had not been in the mood today to get in the cold water. River could tell he had music on his mind. It was too hard to come up with tunes in his head while dismantling a dock. "When inspiration hits, it's hard to stop it," he'd told her many times. Mr. Janson and Mr. Farrington didn't look excited about the job either. They looked slightly annoyed with Mr. Wren. But the dock was out and now they could enjoy a beer. Savannah was transporting her rocks off the other side of the beach from where River sat. She was taking them up the hill, where she'd disappear behind the house and then return again. She'd dug up about ten rocks around that section of birch trees, which had amazed them both. *Why were they there to begin with? I mean, who had buried them?*

"Savannah, where are you putting those rocks? I don't think Mom wants them near the house," River said, banging her sneakers against the metal dock.

"River. Do that again with your sneakers," her dad said. She moved her feet again. "Again." He hummed along with the banging. "Yeah, I think I've got something there. Guys, meet me in the studio in about half an hour." He raced up the hill, disappearing at the same place where Savannah kept reappearing. Joe came walking down the hill and waved at River.

"Want to ride to the gallery with my mom and me? The opening's on Friday. We came by to borrow some tools from your dad." He stopped in front of her and put his hands in his jeans pockets. His shirt had a hole in it, his hair was sticking up in the back, and his wire-framed glasses were smudged. That was Joe. He could be in a band when he grew up.

"What? What are you looking at?" He looked at his outfit.

"You look like you could be in a rock band."

"Thanks!" He pulled out his shirt and examined the tear. "But all our dads don't dress like this, just your dad." He smiled. She smacked him on the shoulder. "That didn't hurt."

"It wasn't supposed to," River said, laughing. "Don't make fun of my dad."

"I'm only kidding."

"I know." They walked up the hill. "Your dad owns the hardware store in town, so you must have all the tools your mom could need at your house."

"Yes. We have a lot of tools," agreed Joe.

"So why is your mom stopping by our house to borrow my dad's tools?"

"Because your dad has better tools."

"Huh? Better tools?"

"Yes," Joe said.

"Whatever," said River, laughing. They were at the car and getting into Mrs. Farrington's Chevy station wagon. River asked Joe's mom what tools she was borrowing. She was curious what amazing tools her dad had that the owner of a hardware store wouldn't carry.

"It's a kind of nail that works best to hang a picture. I've tried different nails, and a kind I found at your house works the best. And wire. For the back of the frames. I like the wire your dad has better than what we have in the store." *Oh.* It wasn't as interesting as River thought it'd be. "I'm also borrowing your mom's Polaroid camera that she uses to take photos of her work."

Savannah giggled from the far back seat, making River jump. "Geez, Savannah." Her sister was holding Scratchy. Scratchy was Joe's cat. He was black on top and all white on the bottom and was High-Five's brother. They'd found the two alone in the woods when they were kittens. Scratchy got his name because that was the first thing he did to Joe when he picked up the small animal: scratch him on the hand. High-Five got his name because the first time River picked him up, he'd held up his left paw like he was "high-fiving" her. Scratchy spent most of his time in the art gallery with Mrs. Farrington. He liked riding in the station wagon, so mom and cat made frequent trips from home to work and back again. Scratchy also seemed to like hanging out in the garage that was attached to the gallery building.

As they pulled up in front of Mrs. Farrington's art gallery, River noticed two large planters with what looked like small pine trees in them. She nodded. They made the front of the building look more inviting. Attached to the side of the art gallery was a large garage. Without the trees, the buildings looked like giant marshmallows. Stepping inside the gallery with Savannah and Scratchy behind her, River noticed the walls were still painted an avocado color, like the kitchen appliances in her house. She didn't care for the popular color. Scratchy went over to sniff one of the paintings that was lined up next to the others against the walls in the order they'd be hung. Joe and his mom went back to the car to bring in the final things needed to install the exhibit. Savannah twirled in the center of the room; River followed the cat and began looking at the paintings of Lenape women and men. Her heart beat fast as she knelt in front of the portrait of the Native man that had appeared on the gallery invitation. The artist had painted him from the waist up. *Wow! So neat! This person could be my relative.*

Joe and his mom were putting the supplies on a table near the door. "Mrs. Farrington," asked River, "where did you get the paintings from?"

"They're from an estate sale in Lambertville." She paused. "Your dad is Lenape? Am I correct?"

"Yes," answered River. She studied the man in the picture. Did he look like her dad? *Was* one of these a painting of her relative? She had tears in her eyes, but she didn't want to cry in front of Joe and his mom or her sister. "It's funny. My dad and I were talking about his side of the family recently. I wonder if he knows these paintings are here?"

"I don't know, dear," Mrs. Farrington told her. "You know your dad isn't really into art. Visual art, that is . . ." River smiled and nodded. "No, music's the only art he's interested in." She returned her attention to the painting.

She couldn't tell if it was a person who was alive now or a picture of someone who died a long time ago since the labels had not yet been put with the paintings. River thought that the warm colors around the figure didn't match his expression. He'd lifted his chin so that he looked down on the viewer, but not as if he felt superior. Instead, River imagined that he was judging the artist to see if he would be painted with respect. *I wonder if the artist was a white guy? He probably was.* The Native wore a bright red headpiece with gray and white feathers sticking out of it. From his ears hung spectacular earrings, maybe made out of silver. The white tie around his neck reminded her of a bow on one of her mom's blouses. River loved how his red coat with gold trim matched the headpiece. He was holding something that looked like wood, with carving and a circle at the top. He drew her in with his intense gaze. She felt proud—he must be her ancestor.

She moved from painting to painting. No one talked behind her. All she heard were things being moved around. Even Savannah was quiet, which was unusual. The next painting she stopped at was a portrait of a beautiful woman with black hair and brown eyes. Butterflies fluttered around her head. She was wearing beads and a shawl, with two huge feathers in her hair attached by a bejeweled butterfly barrette. River wondered what bird they'd come from. Her expression was sad. One hand was against her cheek, the other held a bouquet of daisies. River moved in closer to see what was on top of the flowers. It was a pendant with a silver frame that encased a jade turtle. River loved the shape of the turtle. *I wonder what the turtle means to the Lenape?* She stood back and took in the portrait. River put her hands to her mouth.

"I think she looks like you," said Mrs. Farrington.

River's cheeks became warm. "I don't know if I'll ever be as pretty as she is."

"She may be your relative." Mrs. Farrington put her hand on River's shoulder.

River's head ached from happiness. The scent of the bowl of strawberry potpourri Mrs. Farrington had on a small table by the front door filled her nose. River didn't care for the sweet aroma. It brought her out of the spell the paintings had put her in, and made her remember she was there to help out. She asked what she could do and then asked to place the labels in front of the artwork. The paintings had been painted by different artists between 1967 and the present time. After she'd completed her job, she got up and headed into the garage to move away from the smell. In one corner of the large room, she walked around tables covered with stacks of other paintings the gallery sold, empty picture frames, nails, and hammers.

The room needed organizing. It needed shelves to hold the paintings. Scratchy followed her around the room by jumping up on each table and down again. Mrs. Farrington had explained her collection was by local and regional artists. At the garage door, River picked up the cat. "I have an idea, Scratchy. I have an idea."

She joined the others back in the gallery, where Savannah was bouncing from one painting to another. "Oh, I like this one! I like this one too. Oh, not that one. He looks so mean!"

"He could be our relative, Savannah," River said.

Savannah stared at the portrait. "He doesn't look like me." She puckered her lips. "He looks like Dad," she said, not making the connection that even though she had completely different hair and eye colors, she was a descendant of the Lenape too.

The next day, after dinner and homework at their own homes, George and Joe went over to River's. The three were now sprawled out on the Wrens' porch reading as rain poured down. River liked a rainy evening. Today it had rained all day. When it rained like this on the weekends, they usually went outside to gather rocks to then paint, and set these pet rocks on the windowsill to dry. Another activity they'd do, with River's mom's help, was make Shrinky Dinks, small plastic shapes that were baked in the oven. There were flowers and animals and smiley faces that the kids were going to make into jewelry or just keep as trinkets.

River's mom was sitting at the kitchen table flipping through craft books for new ideas for using clay. The three could hear her talking to River's dad. "Here's an idea. Ceramic pieces for the wall. Look here. I could make butterflies. Wow, those are bright colors. I don't know if I'd make them so glowing. This smiley face is cute. That'd be great for a kid's room. Oh, and look at this lamb. Now, that would be perfect for a baby's room. Honey, what do you think?"

"Yeah," her dad replied. "Sounds good." His voice wasn't as enthusiastic as her mom's.

Her mom said, "Yes. I think this is what I'm going to do."

River thought the idea was rather boring. Things to hang up in babies' rooms. Her mom made beautiful mugs and tea bowls. Why would she want to spend her time making lamb and smiley-face wall hangings? But she had to make things that would sell. River looked at her friends. They were into their books. She returned to reading Nancy Drew volume number thirty-eight, *The Mystery of the Fire Dragon*, which George had finished yesterday. George was reading an Archie comic book. The Nancy Drew and Hardy Boys series competition that had started in the middle of September was still going on. Along with homework and reading their comic books, they read two novels a month.

Joe was reading something he wasn't supposed to be reading—an Elmore Leonard novel. They were crime books. Joe's mom did not want her thirteen-year-old son to read Elmore Leonard books because of lines like "Are you gonna just stand there or turn the lights out?" Joe would read parts like this to River and George when no adults were nearby. The books didn't really have anything in them that their parents considered "dirty"—and anyway, the scenes Joe read made them giggle. They laughed about how the author never seemed to stop talking about women's legs and other parts of their bodies.

He closed the Leonard paperback and put it in his pile, which also included another series called Encyclopedia Brown, and The Three Investigators, which he'd shown them a while ago at the library.

"So you like this series?" River asked, pointing to the book.

"The Three Investigators? Yes, I do," said Joe. He and the girls looked at the doorway that led from the kitchen to the porch, where River's sister was standing.

Savannah came out wearing her matching blue polka-dot raincoat and boots. She looked like she was trying to sneak past them.

"Where are you going?" asked River. "You're not going outside in the rain, are you? And anyway, it's going to get dark out soon."

"Mom said I could, if I'm quick. And as long as there's no thunder or lightning." She put her hood up and slid out the screen door, letting in the sound of the rain beating on the wood deck.

George looked up from her book. “What’s your sister going to do?”

“I don’t know exactly. She found those rocks. She must be doing something with them.”

Joe laughed. “Maybe she’s going to make her art out there.”

“With rocks?” asked George. “How do you make art with rocks?”

“Don’t know,” said River. “Maybe she’s making something for the fairies.”

“Hey, they have a business card!” Joe said, interrupting his friends’ conversation.

“Who?” said George.

“The kid detectives in this book. They have business cards for their detective agency.”

“They have a card for their detective agency! I don’t believe it!” George said sarcastically.

“And . . . so?” asked River, ignoring George’s comment.

“The three of us could be detectives, and I could make us cards that had the name of the agency with our names. See?” He held up a page that had an illustration of a business card. “‘The Three Investigators,’” Joe read. “‘We Investigate Anything.’ Then it lists the names of the First

Investigator, Second Investigator, and Records and Research."

River laughed. "Joe, why would we form a detective agency? There aren't any mysteries around here."

"Savannah trying to sneak out the door gave me the idea. What if she's up to something? Maybe we should investigate what she's doing. I haven't said anything, but I swear I saw her by the old barn when I was riding home from the hardware store with my dad the other day."

"I'm not sure about that. I don't think she leaves the house without asking my parents first. She doesn't want to get in trouble, especially with my dad. He's the disciplinarian of the two."

"And what possible thing could a nine-year-old be doing that'd be mysterious?"

"I think we should form a detective club. Since we read mystery series," Joe said.

"Since we read kid mystery series we should have a detective club? I don't know if that—"

River interrupted George. "If you want us to be in your detective club, we'll be in your detective club, Joe," she reassured him. "Right, George?" She motioned to her.

"Yes, okay, we will be in your club." Sitting with her legs crossed, George put her chin on her hands. "So how do we start?"

Joe smiled like the sun had found its way through the rain to shine on his face. "Okay. Naturally I'll be . . ."

George leaned over to River. "Are you sure we want to be in this club?"

"Shush," whispered River.

Joe put the book down in front of his crossed legs and creased the page where the picture of the card was. "As I started to say, I will be the first investigator; I nominate River to be the second investigator; and George, you can be the records keeper and researcher."

They waited for George's response. She made them wait a beat. "Okay, I'll be your records keeper and researcher. Do you know what that means?"

"No, not yet, but I'll find out or make something up for you to do." He got up. "I think I'll go home and finish reading the book and start figuring out all the details of the club. It looks like the rain stopped."

When he was out the door George asked River, "Don't you think he should be the records keeper and researcher since he's the one who volunteers in the library?"

"He could have not invited you. We could have a club without you. He could've invited Ralph instead."

"But he'd never do that. Unless there was another position listed in that kid detective book," George said. "See you tomorrow."

The rain had finally stopped that night and River craved fresh air, so she was sitting on the deck in the dark, a beach towel under her. She was thinking about Joe's detective club. It would be fun. They could make up mysteries if they couldn't find any real ones. *Are we too old to play detective?* A person in a speedboat floated by her with its two lights indicating its presence. A gentle wake rolled toward the dock. Once the sun was down, the boats on Lake Saturday were not supposed to make a wake other than the one that was rocking River now. The movement unraveled a thought in River's mind. *Mrs. Janson. Now she was a mystery.*

How could the detective club investigate George's mom? Should just she and Joe investigate what might be going on with her? Definitely all three of them could look into Savannah's actions. But what about Mrs. Janson? Was it inappropriate for kids to get into an adult's business? Especially when it was their best friend's parent?

River had been affected emotionally and physically by George's mom's recent behavior. She had known her all her life and couldn't remember another time when she'd acted the way she had. Although October had gone by, and River hadn't observed any more outbursts from Mrs. Janson. But had George? She returned to the idea of an investigation.

How could River find out why Mrs. Janson had acted the way she had? River watched the surface of the lake become still again. Soon there wouldn't be boats on the water, as the month went on. And as September had turned into October and now it was the beginning of November, River had begun to realize that it really bothered her that her friend had to live with a mom like Mrs. Janson. She was starting to worry about George. River had seen and experienced how uncomfortable and even scary it was to be around a person like George's mom. But how could she find out? Then she remembered that Joe had an older sister, Beth, who was a nurse. Maybe that's where she and Joe (and George?) could begin.

It was four o'clock on Friday, three hours before the gallery opening. River held a clipboard with the list of artists, titles of the paintings, and prices. She'd been asked to check that Mrs. Farrington's list was in the same order as the artwork on the wall. Then Joe would have it during the opening and be the contact that the gallery attendees would go to if they wanted information about one of the paintings. Mr. Farrington was in charge of the drink and food table set up at the back of the gallery next to the door to the garage. They offered sodas and water, wine for the adults, and cheese and crackers and fruit. Savannah was to make sure the plates of food stayed full. River would be a hostess directing the guests to the refreshments or to Joe for questions about the artwork. George was in bed with a bad cold and had made it clear to

River that she was annoyed. She didn't like missing out on anything.

Shortly after seven, the guests began trickling in. River listened to the oohs and aahs the people made as they moved from painting to painting. As the gallery continued to fill, she walked around eavesdropping on people's comments about the portraits. *About my people.* She stepped behind a couple she didn't know but had seen at Market Day. She listened to the woman say, "Look at that funny neck-thing he's wearing. He's so serious. A lot of their expressions are so down. Why can't they smile?"

A man next to them said, "I would consider buying one if they had pleasanter expressions." The couple nodded. "But," he continued, "I may be buying one anyway—my wife's in love with the woman with the butterflies." River's heart began beating fast. *Oh no.* She was conflicted. She wanted the painting to remain in the gallery, but the paintings were for sale and so the best thing would be if it sold. And the husband said his wife wanted it, so it would be treasured. At least River hoped it would be.

Mrs. Farrington came up to River. She may have seen her leaning in to hear the reactions to the paintings. "Some people are finding the portraits beautiful and stoic." She patted River. "Many people have great respect for the Lenape tribe. You should be proud." River smiled at her. Joe's mom was a very sweet lady. And it was cool that she was having an exhibit of this artwork.

She scanned the room. Savannah was stationed beside the food and drink table giving a serious look to a woman filling her plate. Her mom was chatting with a woman River didn't recognize, and her dad was by himself in a corner. Her opportunity had presented itself. He was looking at his glass of red wine, probably wishing Mrs. Farrington would've offered him a beer instead. River remembered her dad saying numerous times how expensive renting a garage out for his shop was becoming, and that it wasn't close to their house. So River had come up with an idea.

"What do you think of the paintings, Dad?" She stood close to her dad.

"They're . . ." He seemed to be struggling to figure out what to say.

"I think they're grand." That was a word River rarely used, if ever, but it came to her and seemed to be the right one.

"I guess," said her dad. Savannah ran up to them.

"Dad! Did you see the guy who looks like you?" River wondered if her dad thought her sister meant a person in the room.

"Who looks like me?" He looked around the room. River held her breath.

"The man in that portrait over there. With the bright red headpiece with feathers sticking out of it and the huge earrings!" Savannah took his hand. "Come on. I'll show you." The two walked away.

Joe walked up to them. "We've had some people very interested in buying! I heard a lady say to her husband that portraits like these are becoming more and more popular!"

River asked, "Did the portrait of the Lenape woman with the butterflies sell?"

"Yes! That was the first one to sell." His cheerfulness calmed River's anxiety. *Why is my stomach hurting?* It was a lot to get used to: beginning to feel connected to her heritage while at the same time seeing such powerful and meaningful images of her people being sold to non-Natives who may not appreciate them.

River joined her mom, who was talking with Mrs. Janson. Attempting to not be obvious, she studied her mom's face. Her greenish-blue eyes were pretty with her pale skin color. Her mom's reddish-brown hair wasn't shiny black like River's, but River liked how strands of flaming red came out when the sun shone on her mom's hair. The two women were deep in conversation about wall colors, so River went back to her dad.

"Dad, can I show you something in the garage?" He was standing by himself again.

He followed her to the door of the garage. As she opened the door, Scratchy bounded out. "No you don't!" River picked him up and carried the cat back into the garage.

The corner of the garage River and Scratchy had visited earlier in the week looked the same, though there were fewer paintings stacked on the tables and one of the tables was empty. River's dad stood in the entrance and looked in her direction. "Look," said River, holding out her arms. "Look how large it is."

"Mrs. Farrington needs shelves for these paintings. And her workstation is a mess," Mr. Wren said. "What did you want to show me?"

River looked at the floor, feeling anxious for a moment. Her parents did not talk with her about family finances. There was no reason to. They provided everything she and Savannah needed and more. River wasn't sure how her dad would react to her suggestion. *But it's such a good idea!* So she went with it. "This is really a large space. It's a garage, actually!" She pointed to the gigantic garage door. "It's the size of *your* repair shop." She paused. "I've heard you and Mom talking about the rent increasing for your repair shop, and how you're tired of the drive out there. So, I thought maybe you could rent this space from Joe's mom." She watched her dad take in the cavernous room, with a window on the left and one at the far end. She brought her dad to the middle of the room and said, "Maybe this wall over here by the door could be made into a room for shelves for the gallery. And it wouldn't take too much space from your area to work on your cars." She crossed her arms, satisfied with her sales pitch.

Her dad had crossed his arms and was looking around. Then he nodded, and River's heart beat faster. "Hmm. River, you might have an idea here." He squinted at her. "Did you tell Mrs. Farrington about your idea?"

"No. I was thinking of you. But *really*, you like the idea?"

"If you made that into a room for the art things, it'd be easy to make shelves . . . this certainly looks like the size of my repair shop." He nodded again. "Have to think about it. And figure out what I can afford and if Mrs. Farrington would even be willing or interested in renting out this space, especially for a repair shop. I don't know."

"You have the neatest and cleanest repair shop I've ever been in, Dad."

He chuckled. "It's the *only* repair shop you've been in. But you are right about that. Crazy idea. But maybe . . ." He looked at his watch. "Time to go."

Heading toward the door to the gallery, he patted River's shoulder as he passed.

Yes! Maybe she had helped her dad.

The weekend before Thanksgiving River and Joe planned to talk with his sister, Beth, hoping that since she was a nurse she might be knowledgeable about different types of behavior and why someone would act certain ways. She lived in Maryland with her husband and kids. Joe had told River that his sister called his parents every Sunday. River had filled Joe in on the behavior of Mrs. Janson that she witnessed on the library trip and in the kitchen. Joe expressed to River that there might not be anything abnormal about George's mom's reactions. River told him that the bad feeling she'd had about the situations wasn't going away. So Joe reassured her he was going to help out however he could.

Earlier than needed, River went over to Joe's house, which was across the lake. River could walk to his house either by passing George's place or going around the other way, which is how she went. She hadn't had the chance to let Joe know she wanted to come over early and hoped he was there and hadn't gone to Mrs. Farrington's art gallery or Mr. Farrington's hardware store. When she saw the family car gone but Scratchy in hunter mode in front of a tree with a squirrel in it, she figured at least Mrs. Farrington was home. Maybe she could somehow bring up speaking with her daughter.

"Hi, Mrs. Farrington. Is Joe here?" She walked into the house and into the office where Joe's mom was sitting at the desk with files in front of her.

"Hi, River. Joe will be back very soon. He's helping his dad at the store." She looked at her watch. "He said he must be back at four for your first meeting." She smiled at River. "He seems very serious about this detective club."

"Actually, I'm here hoping to talk to Beth when she calls," explained River.

"Oh?" She was running her pencil down a list of figures, then stopped. "You want to speak with Beth?" She had River's full attention. "I'm sorry, hon, but Beth's not calling tonight. Next weekend she will. Is there anything I can help you with?"

"No, thank you, Mrs.—Joe, you're back. You're mom said Beth isn't calling tonight. Maybe we can have that first investigators meeting. George is home, I think."

"Sure!" said Joe. "I'll call her. I already have everything set up on the floor in my room."

"Of course you do, Joe," said River, chuckling.

About fifteen minutes later, George arrived and they went into Joe's room, where there were three blue beanbags, each with a folder in front of it. "Sit on the beanbag with the folder that has your name on it." George jumped on the bag with the "River" folder. River took George's spot. "Give me a break, will ya?" Joe said. So they gave him a break and exchanged seats. He sat in his self-assigned seat between them. "Now we'll count to three, and then open our folders."

Joe started: "One-" Then the girls chimed in with "Two-three-go!" and they flipped their folders open. "Oh!" River and George exclaimed. "This is cool, Joe!" Inside the folders, Joe had put together papers he'd typed along with his much-anticipated business cards secured with a paper clip with their club's official name, "Three Detectives Club." What River especially liked was the Hardy Boys–blue and Nancy Drew–yellow buttons with their names and titles on them, which had fallen out into their laps when they'd opened their folders.

"It has my name on it!" said George. "George Janson, Recorder and Researcher." She clipped the shiny button to her peasant blouse.

"Mine too! 'River Wren, Second Investigator.'" River attached it to her pine-green T-shirt that had "Give a Hoot, Don't Pollute" on the front.

Joe's cheeks were flaming red. "My dad has a button maker in the store." He waited a moment for them to calm down. "Now, the first sheet—"

"You typed all these sheets, Joe?" George said. "I don't even know how to type!" She nudged River. "He works in the library and knows how to type. Are you really thirteen, Joe? Or are you a thirty-year-old man under that shirt?"

Joe's cheeks flushed again. He pulled his shirt collar up. "I volunteer at the library. I'm too young to be paid. Now, as I started saying." He looked at George, then at River. "As I started to say, the first sheet is a description of each of our jobs. I won't read them now. You can read them when you're home. The next page is a glossary of some of the terms detectives commonly use while investigating. Do you have any questions about them now?" They all looked down at the eighteen vocabulary words.

"Is battery the same thing as assault?" asked George.

"Good question," replied Joe. "An assault is an unlawful attempt or threat to harm someone."

"Oh," said River. "I hope we aren't going to be dealing with assault."

Joe shook his head. "I'm sure we won't be dealing with assault."

"Good," said George. She sat back in her beanbag.

"I typed up several copies of page number three. It's our case form." He paused for the other two to consider the seriousness of this club. "Again, the purpose of the Three Detectives Club is to find and solve mysteries. Everyone on board?"

"Sounds cool," replied George. "I'm on board. River?"

"I am too." She looked at the last sheet. It had Savannah's name at the top followed by "Case #1." "So, my sister is our first mystery case? Do you really think she's doing something mysterious?"

"You don't seriously think she's doing anything wrong or has done anything illegal, do you, Joe? Savannah's only nine," said George.

"Have we not been reading Hardy Boys and Nancy Drew books since we learned to read? And aren't most of the cases nothing like the things that happen in Elmore Leonard books?" asked Joe.

"I sure hope I don't have to see any women's legs coming out from pink bathrobes!" George laughed. Then River laughed, and Joe did too.

"Maybe someday we'll come across an actual dangerous assignment, but for the beginning of our club let's concentrate on whether or not a nine-year-old girl is up to something curious. If that's okay with you, River. We won't investigate if you don't want us to."

"I'm becoming interested. And I don't want her to hurt herself or get into trouble with our parents. And if you did see her by herself around the old barn, well, that could be dangerous if a rotted beam fell on her." River's heart tightened. "I hope she's not hanging out in there."

"I'm sure she's not. But it'll get us started on how we begin investigating a case, right, Joe?" said George.

"Right! That's right, George!" Joe leaned forward and the other two did the same. "Now, I think we should make a plan for how to begin finding out if Savannah is up to anything mysterious."

They spent an hour putting together a plan that would begin tomorrow after school.

That night River woke up and rolled over on her side, knocking High-Five off the bed. "Sorry, High-Five." She'd been dreaming. What had she been dreaming about? She'd been in the woods and someone had been walking behind her. She'd been carrying something, a piece of paper.

She looked into the darkness to where her desk was. The case sheet! She'd been carrying a case sheet. And it had been Mrs. Janson who had crept up behind her and said "Boo!" River sat up and turned on the lamp on the bedside table. A stack of Nancy Drew books lay there. "I need to read something other than these." Maybe there was a book on the bookshelf in the family room that she'd want to read.

She got out of bed, put on her robe, and went out to the family room. She turned on the closest lamp and trotted over to the built-in bookcase her dad had made. She switched on a wall sconce next to it. River scanned the row of books. Her finger stopped at the title *The Country of the Pointed Firs* by Sarah Orne Jewett. She pulled it out and placed it on the chair next to the shelf. Next to it was a narrow spine with the title *Lenni-Lenape Tribes.* She pulled out the small book and opened it. The pages of the book were a bit worn. It had been read. *Whose book is it?* She couldn't imagine her dad buying or reading this book. She looked at the copyright page. It was the same year her dad had been born. She felt tears forming. River turned to the title page and read, "To my son, your heritage is sacred and forever with you. Love, Your Mother and Father." Her chest warmed. Her dad's parents had died before she'd been born. She touched her grandmother's handwriting. She wiped the tears on her cheeks. She took the two books, *Lenni-Lenape Tribes* and *The Country of the Pointed Firs,* back to her bedroom and put them on top of the nightstand, turned off the light, and fell back asleep.

That week River read *Lenni-Lenape Tribes* and began reading *The Country of the Pointed Firs* while on Thanksgiving break. She still felt emotional from the night she'd pulled the book from the bookshelf, and she felt relieved when she was on the last page and could begin the other book. What she thought of now as her dad's book didn't have a lot of information in it about the tribe. It had beautiful watercolor illustrations portraying families working together to construct shelters and to prepare a deer to use for food and clothing. The text explained what was obviously shown in the pictures. The book was a little disappointing to River because it didn't show or tell her anything different from what she'd seen and heard in school. What was magical about it was that it had been given to her dad when he was an infant. She was thankful for her dad, as well as the rest of her family and her friends.

On Sunday, she was going with the plan she and Joe had agreed on: speaking to Joe's sister, Beth, to try to find out anything about Mrs. Janson's behavior that might help George. She was bringing a notepad and pencil with her to Joe's. It worked out that they were speaking with her today because the family had talked with her on Thanksgiving three days ago. "Beth doesn't like to miss a Sunday!" Mrs. Farrington had told River. "We won't have much to talk about, so more time for you and Joe." They had made up a school assignment that involved picking a state where you knew someone and talking to them about it.

She walked past Savannah sitting in front of the TV in the family room. She was having a good morning, having found one of her favorite cartoons, *The Jetsons,* on TV. She was mimicking Mrs. Jetson in a high voice. "'I just turn the Dial-a-Meal to fried chicken, press the button, and it comes out a pill!' Hey!" she yelled. "Mrs. Janson looks like Mrs. Jetson! Mrs. Jetson and Mrs. Janson are so pretty!"

River's shoulders fell. *Why should I feel it's my job to find out if something's wrong with my best friend's mom?* She was confused. She was curious to learn about mental health issues. She wanted to help, but if she found out what was happening to Mrs. Janson, then *how* could she help her or George?

When it was time to go, she said see you later to her parents and headed to the Farringtons' place. As she approached the front door she stopped. Her stomach hurt. She was nervous. The door swung open and Joe greeted her. Laughter came from the kitchen, along with warm light shining down from the chandelier. Joe's mom was sitting on a stool with the phone receiver against her ear. She waved River over. "Beth, River just walked in. Do you still have a minute to talk to her? Okay, here she is and Joe again." Joe took the phone and dragged the cord into his bedroom and closed the door. "Told Mom we wouldn't disturb her and would come in here to talk about *Maryland*." Joe held the receiver so he and River could hear his sister. The three chatted about school and the weather, then River spoke up.

"So, Beth. I was wondering if you could give us the name of a medical dictionary?" She made the signal for Joe to get pencil and paper ready. "Okay, I'm ready. The *Oxford Dictionary of Psychology*. Start with that one? Thanks. So, I wanted to talk with you because you're a nurse. You're the only one Joe and I know who's in a medical field. See, the mom of a friend of ours—I'd rather not say who—has been acting strange or different. There have been two times . . ." River described what she remembered about each incident. "Does she scare me? Not right now. She's been acting normal lately when I've been around her. I'm probably overreacting. I probably am." River's cheeks felt warm. "I know. Don't ignore my gut feelings." Joe was still sharing the receiver with her and hadn't said anything.

"Maybe we need to talk to one of the parents?" he asked Beth. They listened to her answer.

"I agree," said River. "I don't think they'll like us prying into another family's business either. That's why we're doing it as a case! Yes, did Joe tell you about our Three Detectives Club? He did? That's how we're justifying getting into other people's business. Do I hear your kids?" Beth told them she'd talk with them anytime and try to answer any questions, and asked them to keep her updated.

"Truance!" Joe shouted as they heard Beth hang up.

"Ouch! Joe, that was right in my ear."

"Why did Truance leave? She left home when she was sixteen, right?"

"Yes. But we're not talking about George's sister."

"Do they know where she is? Do you think she lives nearby? I bet she lives somewhere around here and has been spying on us all these years."

"First of all, you need to stop being obsessed with crimes and mystery stories."

"Let me explain a possible connection." Joe took his time saying each word. "I am saying that if there is something wrong with Mrs. Janson, then whatever is wrong with her could be the reason that Truance left. Unless . . . Before these two incidents, how would you describe George's mom?"

"Well, I've been thinking back as far back as I can, and I've always thought of her as a dramatic person. She dresses like a lady in a commercial selling a fancy car. Or like a lady selling a new refrigerator in a 1950s ad. You know what I mean? Sometimes I thought she was just acting like she was one of those women in those advertisements. But then in September, when we went to the library, she had us walk through the woods. And it was an awful day. It'd rained the day before. It was muddy and cold. It was strange to me. It seemed out of character for Mrs. Janson."

"That does sound a bit odd," said Joe.

"And how she was acting, and what she was wearing. George told me that it was Mrs. Janson's idea to walk through the woods to the library: not in a car, not along the road, but *through the woods*—and when she decided that was what we were going to do, how did she dress? She wore an expensive coat and dress and heels and carried her fancy leather purse. It just didn't make sense," said River.

"Maybe she's just eccentric. I haven't paid attention to how she acts. She's always just been another adult to me."

"Her mood changed," River continued, unable to get her mind away from the event. "She was all happy, almost skipping along to the library, then when we got ready to leave, George asked if we could please walk home by the road. And her mom became sad, so suddenly. It was eerie. She dragged herself back home. Why should she be so upset with us wanting to walk along the road so we don't get muddy again? Our moms wouldn't act like that!"

"What about the Tupperware incident?" Joe asked. Scratchy came into the room and walked over to him, then decided to visit River.

"She did scare me. She was throwing the Tupperware at the cupboard. So mad. And at what? Most people's kitchen cupboards are unorganized and cluttered. There isn't a plastic container or pot or pan in the world that hasn't tumbled out of its cupboard at least once!" she said, petting the cat.

Joe chuckled. "That's true. I remember hearing my dad say that George's mom was 'quirky.'"

"Really? That's interesting," said River, looking at Scratchy purring in her lap.

"Well, my dad is the straight man in the band, you remember. He thinks most people are quirky."

They sat in silence, watching the cat.

"River," said Joe. "I think you should wait and see about Mrs. Janson. See if she does anything else strange. You could record her behavior. Keep a journal. That's a good idea!"

"And that's not creepy at all, Joe!"

He ignored her comment. "Have you told George?"

River waved her hands. "No! She doesn't want to talk about it. I can tell."

Joe nodded. "Sounds like her. . . . But now I think we have another mystery to solve. I think I need to fill out another Three Detectives Club form for our files." He reached over to a pile of files on the floor by his desk.

River grinned. "We have *files*?"

"We are a serious club. We are going to be solving mysteries." He handed the files to her.

"What is the other mystery going on file now?" She opened the top one and saw it was Savannah's investigation.

"So, we have Savannah's, then the mystery of Mrs. Janson's odd behavior, and now the mystery of where Truance Janson is."

"One at a time, I'd say." River got up with Scratchy in her hands. He immediately escaped and went out of the room. "Thank you, Joe. Thanks for listening to me and letting me talk to Beth. I know I don't have any business prying into George's family, but I just—her mom's behavior bothers me. I'm curious why she acts the way she does sometimes." She laughed. "I read way too many mysteries too." As they headed out the side door of Joe's house, they saw George running toward them.

"River! Joe!" she yelled. "I think Savannah's sneaking out! C'mon, let's follow her!"

The three ran from Joe's house to the side of George's house where they stopped to watch a petite figure in a red hooded winter coat and brown boots walk to the road that their houses were on and that led to the old barn, look both ways, then cross it.

"Do you think she's going to the barn?" asked George.

"Maybe. Wait till she's a little farther down the road," said Joe. They waited a moment and then he said, "Let's go."

River's heart pumped fast. It was exciting following a "suspicious person"—even if the person was a nine-year-old girl named Savannah who'd probably just found a hiding place for her stupid rocks. Why she would take them to the old barn *was* a mystery though, and it wasn't a safe place to play in. So it would be worthwhile, if that's where she was going, to stop her from playing in there.

The team moved out at a safe distance and began tracking the small figure in red. There weren't many trees to hide behind along the road. But Joe was the leader, and he kept his partners in line with him so, as he said, "We'll look less conspicuous." The wind was having fun with River's friends. It was teasing George's hair, flipping it into her face, and swirling dirt onto Joe's glasses. "Stop it," River whispered. She liked it; the wind was blowing a nice cool breeze against her neck.

Savannah seemed to be heading to the old barn. Joe motioned for River and George to stop. "Let's just wait here. There isn't any other place she could be going except to where we thought she'd go." He stepped back and turned to them. "So, how do you like your first—"

"Stalking?" George said. "It's pretty exciting. Although this wind . . ." She grabbed her hair again and tucked it in her sweatshirt.

"We are following someone. Like a car tails another car in TV shows."

"Wow," said George. "Wait until Savannah starts driving, then we'll really have a chase!"

River looked in the direction Savannah had gone. Enough time had passed for her to have reached the building. "Should we continue walking?" she suggested.

"Okay. Come on," said Joe. "Now, watch your feet. Try not to step on any twigs."

They went step by step, looking at the ground before they placed their feet.

"This is kinda fun!" whispered George to River. River wanted to say it was a lot more fun than walking with George's mom to the library.

They reached the barn and saw a vacant entry into darkness. Joe went first, then River, then George. As the last member of the Three Detectives Club made her way over the threshold, they heard a loud giggle and a trampling of leaves. They ran through the barn. There was another door on the other side! The three rushed out the back door to see Savannah in her red coat and dark boots running into the woods, back to Lake Saturday. She was flailing her arms like she was going to fly, and she was laughing. River frowned at her sister, who looked like a garden gnome.

George smacked Joe's shoulder. "Ouch!" he said.

"You let a nine-year-old make fools of us!" said George.

"How'd she know?" asked River. "How'd she know we were following her?"

Joe had an astonished expression. "She set us up! Wow. She's sneaky. She knew we were on to her!" River and George laughed. "What?" Joe asked.

"She's not that clever, Joe, I assure you," said River.

"Savannah must have seen us hiding back at your house, Joe," George said. "Too bad. Looks like she's not doing anything mysterious."

"How do you know?" Joe had his hands on his hips. "I think you're underestimating her."

"Look," said River. She held out a shiny circle. "My button."

"Your Three Detectives Club badge!" Joe frowned at River. "You're supposed to take care of it, not let some misfit take it from you." He looked at George, then down at his own coat. "We should all be wearing our badges."

"You *are* cute sometimes, Joe," George said, and put her hand on his shoulder. River thought Joe might die on the spot. On cue his cheeks turned blistering red.

Joe straightened his back and said, "Savannah knows about our group now. That compromises our investigation."

"Maybe not," said River. They had returned to the middle of the barn. "Let's look around. Maybe there's a clue as to why my sister is coming here, if she's coming here."

"But if she knows we're investigating her, she'll act differently and she could conceal evidence from us."

George had wandered off to a corner of the barn. River could tell from her posture that she was suppressing a laugh.

"Let's walk around and see if we find anything," River said to Joe.

The three were on different sides of the barn. Sunlight shone through cracks in the boards. A bird fluttered in the loft, then flew out the window. The inside of the barn smelled sweet. The wood was dry, and River inspected the rusted nails along the walls. The aroma was interesting to her. Why would it smell sweet? Piles of wood were scattered around. River approached the one in front of her, which was stacked higher than the others. As she stepped around the pile, she saw a table. It looked like it was made of the same wood as the barn and the wood piles. On top on the left side were autumn leaves and twigs and white branches with gray-brown streaks—the leaves and bark of a birch tree. In the center was a frame made from branches of another tree, and beside it were additional branches. The inside of the branch frame was empty. River heard George and Joe approach from behind.

"What's this?" asked George.

"Did Savannah make this?" Joe asked River.

"I don't know," answered River. "My first thought is she didn't make this."

"Why?" questioned George.

"It seems too organized for her." She picked up a leaf by the stem and twirled it. "I think if she was making pictures with leaves she'd use the ground, not a table."

"Interesting," commented Joe. He made the motion of putting on an imaginary sleuth hat and walked around the table. "I wonder if Savannah knows about the table. It's kind of hidden. Where was your button, River?"

"I found it in the center of the room." She put the leaf down and put her hand on the frame. It was the same size as the ones on the Lenape portraits. "Someone else may be using the barn, for making art."

"Art?" George said. "What art would be made from leaves and branches?"

"I don't know," said River. "Someone made a frame, and gathered leaves and branches and twigs. Put them on this table. It looks like they were going to make a picture."

"So then it must be Savannah. Why would an adult want to play around with this?"

"Maybe it's a modern art artist!" Joe yelled, making the girls jump.

"A what?" asked George.

"My mom has a stack of art magazines. I started looking through them the other day because I'd read all of my comic books. I saw an article on modern art. The art is called Earth art. The artists use natural materials like these." He picked up a handful of leaves.

"You probably shouldn't pick those up, Joe. The artist who's coming back wouldn't want them moved . . . Hmm. So, leaves and branches next to a frame made of branches are materials for modern art," George noted. "I think I might like art made from these things."

"Really?" River asked.

"Yes, I do," George said.

"I'm getting cold," announced Joe. "Mind if we go back?"

"We have a mystery here," River said. "That's cool."

"I'd say we have a mystery here!" George said. She looked at Joe. "Now let's go home."

They left the barn and headed back. First stop was George's house where River and Joe said, "See ya!" and then the two moved on to River's house, where they stood by her front door.

"Are we still planning to go to the library," Joe asked River, "to search through the *Dictionary of Psychology* and any other books on psychology they might have? Tuesday after school we could go since it's my volunteer day."

"The library on Tuesday." River nodded. "Sounds good."

The librarian, who had a little chain attached to her reading glasses, directed them to the reference books and textbooks she had told Joe about. She held up *Psychology: The Briefer Course* by William James. "Here's one I just came upon that might interest you. Then over here is . . ."

The librarian eventually left them, and River opened the thick book and read aloud from the table of contents. "'Chapter One: Habit, Chapter

Two: The Stream of Consciousness.'" The list went: the self, attention, conception, discrimination, and ended with Chapter Seventeen: Will. River closed the book. "I don't think this will help us. I'm impressed she thinks we'd be able to understand this, but . . ." Joe agreed. River turned to the glossary in the next book and ran her finger down the list. "'Behaviorism, Conditioning, Ego, Eugenics.'" She flipped through pages and stopped at the words beginning with *psych*. "'Psychiatry, Psychoanalysis, Psycho-path-ology, Psychotherapy.' Oh, Joe. This is no help. I wouldn't know where to start. This is way over my head." She returned the book to the shelf. The two sat on the floor.

"Sorry, River." He leaned against the books. "The dictionaries are no help either."

"Mrs. Janson's moods change quickly. She can be happy and then sad and then mad in a matter of moments. You don't know what mood she will be in. It could be her birthday and she would be having a great time. George would bring out her birthday cake with candles lit and set it in front of her mom. Most people would smile as their friends and family sang 'Happy Birthday,' then blow out the candles. But for no reason you can see, Mrs.

Janson might suddenly jump up and run out of the room. Then later she'd return to the room, acting like nothing happened. It's how she acts. Her personality is like a swing going up and down. So . . ." She pulled out the book again. "*Per-*, *person-*, here, *personality disorder.* 'A category of mental disorders, with onset no later than early childhood, characterized by pervasive, inflexible, and enduring patterns' . . . Hmm. That doesn't mean anything to me. To you?"

"No," said Joe, standing up. "I've got to get back to work. And sorry we didn't get anywhere with a diagnosis. Maybe you should talk with Beth again. She could explain it to us so we understand."

"If she knows anything about these things." River stood up and said, "Later." On her walk home in the cool fall wind, she convinced herself that what was wrong with George's mom was too complicated for her or Joe to figure out. River frowned. *Even if Beth could tell us what's ailing Mrs. Janson, what would we do then? Would it be enough to have some answers or ideas as to what her condition might be? How would it help George?* She kicked some dirt. *It's not like we could do anything with the information Beth might give us! It's probably a waste of time!*

River said out loud to the sun and the clouds and the trees and the rabbit that'd hopped out of its shelter: "The last day of November. What will the winter bring us? Huh, little one? More mysteries? More questions? Any answers?"

JANUARY

It was Saturday afternoon and the members of the Three Detectives Club, hurried to the door on the side of the Jansons' garage, where Beowulf's Brother was practicing. A snowstorm was coming. Mrs. Wren was snug in her studio-shed working on her new clay wall hangings. After George and Joe shuffled in, River, the last one in, shut the door with gusto. "Wow. The wind is getting ready for the snow," she said. *The wind has to build its strength so that it can blow the snow about. It certainly doesn't want the falling snow to have all the fun.*

River heard her dad's band members say they were working on a love song. She squinted, waiting for his response. "Love song! Beowulf's Brother does not do love songs!" But the other members ignored their leader and plunged into what they'd been working on, and the room began filling with music.

The Three Detectives Club had agreed to have a quick meeting before enjoying their dads' practice. They had not worked on any cases the last month because of too much school work and not wanting to work on any over the holiday break. Now that it was the middle of January, they felt they had to get back to spending time on their cases.

"Okay," said Joe, beginning the meeting. "Where are we? George."

George flipped to her notes. "We have visited the old barn two more times. The second time we noticed that the birch leaves, twigs, and branches were not there. We did not find them inside the barn. They could be outside the barn, but of course we couldn't find them because they're . . . well, they look the same as all the other birch leaves, twigs, and branches out there."

The space was small and it was nearly impossible to have a conversation while the band was practicing, but the kids were used to it and managed to hear each other. George looked back at her notes. "Instead, there were oak leaves and pine needles on the table. The frame was no longer there. It appears that someone is doing something with these materials. Savannah's coming over."

"Hi!" She plunked herself onto River's lap.

"Sit beside me or go back to Mom. You're too old to sit on me." Savannah pouted, then sat where she was told.

"Well," said George looking at Savannah, then at River and Joe, "I think that's all we have for now." She closed her notebook and put the pen in her coat pocket. And they turned their attention to sound of the band.

Beowulf's Brother was getting the new tune down now. They were almost playing it all the way through. "Stop!" Mr. Wren shouted. "It's D minor! D minor!" He made an up-and-down motion with a pick across the guitar strings. River had watched her dad play guitar all her life. The forceful rhythm of the heavy metal music soothed her. But now she was realizing that something else besides her dad's music was a part of her life—her Lenape heritage. She looked at her dad. She'd assumed he'd gotten his musical taste from her uncle, because River's dad had mentioned that the record player in the house was his brother's, and some of the hard rock albums were too.

"Was he in a band?" River had asked her dad.

"No," he'd answered her.

"Did he ever watch you play?"

Her dad squinted. "Maybe. I think when the band first started."

Now she wondered if her dad and uncle had ever heard music from the Lenape tribe. *What does the Native music sound like?* Had they attended any events? Any powwows? She could ask her dad, but she decided to put that on her growing mental list of things she now wanted to find out about her heritage.

"They're done," said George, as she nudged River. "What were you thinking about? You looked like you were deep in thought."

River replied with "Nothing." She watched the dads place their instruments in the cases and set the drumsticks aside; judging by the tone of their voices, they seemed to be pleased with their practice. Savannah was near the door; Joe was looking at a piece of equipment River thought was called a wah wah pedal. River's mom walked in wearing boots and her winter coat with the big hood that had faux fur inside it. She stamped her boots on the mat at the door while holding a ceramic piece. “Whoa! Snow’s starting. I closed up the shed.”

River walked over to her mom. “What do you have, Mom?” She took the piece of unfired ceramic from her mom. “Wow, it’s a butterfly.” When it would be fired, River knew that the glazes would be pink, purple, and yellow. She winced at the thought of the bright colors on one of her mom’s pieces that usually had earth tones. The shape was a butterfly, but a bloated butterfly that looked like it would fall off the wall and maybe even injure a child in a crib below it.

“You don’t like it,” said her mom. “What’s wrong with it? It’s not right, is it? It doesn’t look like it could fly. Does it?” She took it from River. “It’s awful. It looks like it’d fall off the wall.”

“It’s not awful,” River said. Her mom was a good artist. River didn’t want her to think she wasn’t good.

“It’s a fat butterfly!” Savannah said, grabbing for it. Their mom held it to her chest.

“If you don’t like this, then you won’t like the lamb. It looks like a lump of dough.”

"Let's see, hon," their dad said. Their mom held it up. "Oh, well, I'm sure you could just . . . maybe make it smaller."

"I tried to make the butterfly smaller and skinnier, but then it wouldn't hang on the wall right." She handed the piece of ceramic to Savannah, who bounced out the door with it.

River had an idea. She remembered the painting at the gallery with the jade turtle in the silver frame that was around the neck of the beautiful Lenape woman. *I still don't know what the significance of the turtle is.* "I know what you could make, Mom. You could make ceramic jewelry like pendants." Her mom didn't hear her since she'd moved back out into the snowy weather.

That evening the snow began to fall just after River and her family finished supper. Her parents were talking in the porch, Savannah was watching TV in the family room, and River was sitting on the bed reading another Nancy Drew book. It was volume number forty-two, *The Phantom of Pine Hill.* The cover showed a white man dressed in what constituted a stereotypical idea of what a Native wears. Nancy stood behind him; both were looking up at a cliff. The man didn't look like River's dad or the portraits of the Lenape tribe members in the exhibit. Reading the book, she knew that the man on the cover was just "dressing like an Indian"—but why did this white guy wearing a costume to pretend to be a Native have to be on the cover? Why not put a Native on the cover instead? She would be interested to see if this was really important to the story as she got to the end—a person who looked like someone from her Irish background dressed as someone from her Lenape background. *And did it matter?* She thought back to the gallery opening and the woman saying, "Look at that funny neck-thing he's wearing." Then her stomach squeezed as she thought about what her sister had said: "He doesn't look like me." She was just a little girl. It was an innocent thing to say, right? She sighed.

River left her book in the bedroom and went into the family room. Savannah had a large piece of paper and pencils strewn around it. She was making long lines up and down the paper.

"What are you drawing?"

"Lines."

"I know they're lines. I asked you what you are drawing." The lines were like tall grass. They looked like they could move. They looked like they swayed the longer River stared at them.

"No," said Savannah, covering her work. "You can't see it."

"Why?" River sat back in her seat.

"Because." Picking up her pencil and pad, she got up and left the room. "You wouldn't understand my art. And don't come into the room to try to peek."

"Okay, okay!" River said. *Is Savannah up to something mysterious? No. What could she possibly be up to?*

The next morning, River and her friends enjoyed the bright sunlight and became little kids in the snow. Standing in a row in River's front yard—which was the beach in the other seasons—they counted to three and fell on their backs. Then they spread out their arms and legs and moved them like windshield wipers. Each rolled up to a standing position and looked back at their creations. Snow angels! Or vampires, as George called them. Or fairies with capes, as Savannah called them. River sat on her knees and ate the snow. George reminded her not to eat yellow snow, which made River laugh.

"We have to get out our sleds next," said George. But first they went to see what the dads were doing.

On the snow-covered beach, the dads were working on making a fire in the pit. River and the others stood around watching her dad stack the logs until George threw a snowball at her, then they all started throwing snowballs at one another, including the dads. River was backing up to the birch tree clump behind her. Leaning back to launch her molded ball of snow, her foot landed on a small, hard object. She tripped and hit her head on one of the birch trees. "Oh!" She sat on the ground, rubbing the back of her head. Her friends walked up to her.

George laughed. "Are you okay?"

She'd fallen over a rock. One of the rocks Savannah had buried, but not very well. "I'm fine.

Savannah, I thought you'd taken all of these rocks to your hiding place."

"Thought I had," Savannah said. "Are you hurt, River?"

"Go play, Savannah. I'm fine."

The three detectives gathered around River. They were good now at passing secret messages by looking at each other. The plan: to see if Savannah takes this new rock to her hiding place, which they were pretty sure was the old barn.

Later in the day, after some sledding, River was sitting on the front stoop knocking the snow off her boots when Savannah walked from the side of the house across the front yard and toward the street. She had a bulge under her coat.

"Where are you going? What do you have inside your jacket? Hey, Savannah!"

Her sister looked at her. "Mom said I could cross the road if I am careful, to feed the birds. There's a bird feeder back there. I'm filling it up. I've got birdseed." This made sense. Some time ago someone had hung a bird feeder. They took turns filling it if the person who put it up forgot. Or maybe he or she wanted the neighbors to share the feeding responsibilities.

River had had her fill of being out in the cold. Hot chocolate was on her mind. The last thing she wanted to do was trudge through the snow after Savannah. *She's just feeding the birds.*

The following Saturday, River was in the car with George and Mrs. Janson. They were going to the much larger General Store that was a half hour away. To get there they drove to the other side of Sourland Mountain. George's mom had decided George needed new snow boots. George really didn't care if she had new ones. She'd told her mom this, but hadn't received a response. River's mom had given her some money and suggested she look for a couple of new turtlenecks. Savannah did not like shopping, so no little sister to bother them.

Mrs. Janson was in a good mood. She was humming along to a song on the radio. She looked in the rearview mirror and smiled at River. George's mom pulled the car into a parking space. Now almost melted, the snow was dirty from the mud on the road, and had been cleared for cars in the parking lot. Mrs. Janson and the girls made their way to the front door of the General Store, heat hitting River's face as she entered the cavernous space. She didn't go directly up the stairs to the clothes section. Rummaging through the vast number of items they carried was her first priority.

She went to the right to the camping supplies; George and her mom went to the left to the home goods area. Mrs. Janson had mentioned she needed some new mixing bowls. "I saw some in a magazine I'd like to get," she said. About twenty minutes later, River made her way up the stairs to the girls' clothing section, her caramel-colored leather, wooden-soled clogs clicking on each step. There were large tables piled with shirts and pants. She moved from item to item, looking at the colors and prints. She decided to get a white shirt, a fire-engine red one, and a striped one that reminded her of a candy cane, only with blue and yellow stripes too.

Turtlenecks in her arms, she met George and her mom in the shoe department.

George was sitting in a folding chair and Mrs. Janson was kneeling in front of her, pulling off one of her daughter's boots. "Do you like these?" she asked. George shrugged. Her mom sighed. "Which ones do you like?" George scanned the four open shoeboxes surrounding her.

"The pea-green ones." River could tell by George's voice that she just wanted to get her mom to stop making her try on boots. She also noticed Mrs. Janson's tense jaw. They went to the counter with the cash register. "Where's the cashier?" asked George's mom, her lips in a tight line.

George looked around. "Someone'll come."

"Well, I don't see anyone!"

River's heartbeat sped up. *Why is she getting upset? Why is it a big deal that a salesperson's not here? It's Saturday. We don't have to be anywhere.*

"You'd think they wouldn't expect us to wait!" She grabbed River's shirts from her and slapped them on top of the shoebox. River opened her mouth to say she had money for them.

Her shoulders lowered as she heard a voice behind her asking if they were ready to check out.

The salesperson smiled. River wondered how many annoying customers like George's mom she dealt with in a day. River let Mrs. Janson buy her clothes. Her mom would reimburse Mrs. Janson. River would make up an excuse for why she didn't use her money. It wasn't a big deal.

River and George kept their heads down as they went out of the store into the parking lot and got into the car. George hesitated before getting in the front seat, glancing at the back door River had just opened. She sighed and got into the passenger seat. Mrs. Janson slammed the trunk and slid into the driver's seat.

On the ride home River kept her eyes on the scene out the window, the land and trees and the birds that flew by. She wanted the trip to go faster. It took less than half an hour, but the uncomfortable atmosphere Mrs. Janson had created in the car made it feel like time was standing still. They could make it back to their neighborhood okay if no one said anything.

"Mom?" asked George. *George just can't resist saying something!* "Why were you rude to the salesperson?" River clasped her hands and put them in front of her heart.

"I wasn't rude," her mom contended.

"Yes, you were, Mom," George said.

Mrs. Janson stared at her daughter. "Well! If you hadn't taken so long to choose your boots, then maybe the salesperson wouldn't have wandered off."

"She didn't wander off. She was the only salesperson up there. You're crazy." River agreed. The whole incident was ridiculous. Her mom was crazy.

River's skin felt paralyzed. She couldn't hear, or feel the beat of her heart. Sound seemed to freeze. She'd never heard George, or any of her friends, call an adult "crazy," let alone a parent. *What should I do?* She could feel her heart again, but she remained motionless.

George had folded her hands and was looking at them. River wanted to touch her friend's arm, but was afraid to. George might slap her hand away.

Mrs. Janson slammed on the brakes, shattering the stillness. The motion flung George forward; her chest hit the glove box. River's head hit the back of the front seat. They were on the side of the road. River could see the Jewetts' barn in the distance. Mrs. Janson got out of the car, letting in a cool wind. George and River shivered.

"What's she doing?" asked River.

"I don't know," said George. "She's freaking out."

"George, look! She's got the bag! She's—she threw it into the field!"

George grabbed the door handle, then removed her hand.

"There!" yelled George's mom as she got back in the car and slammed the door. "Is that crazy enough for you?" She put the car into Drive and jerked it onto the road. River shut her eyes. *Please don't let there be a car behind us.*

The vehicle raced up the hill, swerving twice. The ride ended in the Jansons' driveway. Mrs. Janson got out of the car, then leaned her head back inside. "You can walk home, River." River got out slowly, her body shaking. Tears running down her face, she headed home.

River passed her family's car in the driveway. What would she say to her mom? She rubbed snow on her cheeks to hide the tears before going inside.

"Is that you, River?" her mom asked from the porch. "Did you buy some turtlenecks?" She looked at her daughter. "Are you okay? Your cheeks are so red!"

"It's cold out. . . . The store didn't have any more turtlenecks for girls," River lied. "They're getting more in later this week. Mrs. Janson's going back.

She said she'd pick me up some." She held out the money. "We'll pay her when she gets them." The lies squeezed out the last energy River had left. She went into her bedroom, shut the door, and fell onto her bed.

She laid on her back. High-Five clawed at the door. She got up and brought him in. "I have to go get the bag," she told the cat. Then she'd have to hide the clothes for a couple of days. Her shock over what had happened turned into anger. River never wanted to see George's mom again! What a horrible person! She pulled the covers over her and High-Five. She cried, realizing that she would have to see Mrs. Janson again. *How am I supposed to avoid her? I don't want to see her or George again. Even if George is my best friend. Maybe she shouldn't be my friend anymore. Joe's my friend. The two of us could hang out without George.* River snorted. *Yeah, right. I can't avoid George. She lives on my street. Our families spend a lot of time together. Our dads are in a band. There's no way I can just decide to not see her.* River closed her eyes and fell asleep.

The day after the awful incident, River and George retrieved the shopping bag. The wind was blowing into it, but the shoebox and turtlenecks were still inside. River rolled her shirts and stuffed them under her coat. They were cold. Her body would warm them up soon enough. She thought about Savannah with the birdseed bag bulging from her chest. She shook her head.

"What?" said George. Her voice sounded defensive.

River smiled at her friend. "I was just remembering the other day. Savannah had a bag of birdseed stuffed in her coat. I look the same." George looked relieved and grinned at her.

"So you haven't seen her go to the old barn again?"

"Not since the snowstorm." They headed back up the mountain without talking. River felt a contentment between her and George. She would always be there for George.

As they reached River's house, George waved to her and headed home.

River then sighed, watching her friend, knowing that every time she wore one of the turtlenecks, it would remind her of what had happened that horrible day.

APRIL

It was the kids' spring break and they had just come back from the Party Store—with extra candy and comic books! River walked into the kitchen where she heard her parents discussing the possible opportunity of renting the garage attached to Mrs. Farrington's art gallery. The space could be Mr. Wren's car repair shop. The idea that an art gallery would be connected to a car repair shop was a unique one. River got a soda from the fridge and sat on one of the chairs in the porch with her new *Wonder Woman* comic book. Her dad hadn't yet approached Mrs. Farrington with the proposal. River smiled hearing her parents talk about her idea. *It'll work! I know it will!*

As for Mrs. Wren's work, her wall hangings for children's rooms had been good sellers at the craft shows. She and the girls had gone to a number of shows over the last four months. The bloated butterfly had been slimmed down so it looked half the weight. The lamb that had resembled a lump of dough now had swirls of wool that looked like clouds, with its legs folded under it and its eyes closed in sleep. The smiley face was painted onto a ceramic circle glazed a loud yellow. Mothers, grandmothers, sisters, and aunts gushed over the wall hangings. River began rolling her eyes every time she heard the same comments from the women, over and over again. They sold out at two shows. After these successful shows, River's mom stopped making her mugs and bowls. The last time River had been at Joe's house, Mrs. Farrington had said it was a shame her mom was no longer making her ceramic pieces. "I've always said she could sell them in the gallery for three times what she was selling them for at the craft shows." River would like to convince her mom that her craft was art, not decorative wall hangings.

River had also thought about telling her mom about Mrs. Janson's behavior. But it seemed like tattling. Or it might even seem like she was gossiping. Which were both things her parents had taught her and her sister not to do. She hadn't talked to Beth again. River didn't know what to ask Joe's sister. *What could I possibly ask her? What could I possibly do to help George or Mrs. Janson?* And then there was the fact that it wasn't River's problem. It was George who had to deal with her own mom.

George and River had not spoken about what happened back in January. Since then, River had made a great effort to avoid spending time at George's house. She'd suggested they hang out at Joe's house more, and that had worked. It'd been easy avoiding George's house—until it was George's birthday, and she announced she was having a party.

Two days before the party, George came over to River's house and asked if she wanted to go to the Party Store with her and her mom. After George left, River's mom asked her why she'd said no. "Why didn't you go? It'd be fun picking out the decorations! You go every year."

River lied again. "Joe and I are already working on some decorations as a surprise. I was going over now, actually."

Her mom kissed her on the head. "You're a good friend." River's stomach hurt.

She stuffed construction paper, scissors, tape, ribbon, glue, and glitter into her navy backpack that had "Conserve Water" printed on the back, and jogged over to Joe's house. She explained what she wanted to make and asked if he would help her. He said sure, and she poured out the materials.

They made a long ribbon that they were attaching cut-out triangular flags to, each with a letter on it spelling out "Happy Birthday George."

River looked at Joe. She needed to tell him about the last incident with Mrs. Janson. "I didn't go to the Party Store because I'm avoiding her mom."

Joe studied the flag in his hand with the letter *t* on it. "Did something else happen?" She told him every detail she could remember from their trip to the store. "Wow," was Joe's response when she was finished.

"I know," said River. "And you're the only one I've told."

"We could tell Beth," he suggested.

"I thought of that too. But what would we ask her? We tried reading through those dictionaries and psychology books. We've got no idea of what terms to use. Anyway, I keep telling myself it's not my business. It's not my problem."

"Except that George is your best friend and something is seriously wrong with her mom."

"I know." River shook her head. "That's why I keep trying to figure out what to do . . . and I'm not ready to talk to my mom about it yet." *Could I talk to Dad during our Sunday time?*

The banner looked great. She and Joe walked it to George's house on her birthday. River's mom would bring the presents. The three families always came together for birthdays. The celebrations started at five o'clock, happy hour for the adults. The Janson house was the nicest of the three homes. Being a carpenter by trade, Mr. Janson was continually remodeling the interior. Mrs. Janson would point out what he'd just finished and what his next project would be. Mr. Janson never looked excited about hearing what he was going to do next.

River had observed the different relationships of the parents, how each couple behaved together. Her parents were very affectionate, sometimes embarrassing her. Joe's parents were more like partners. River had never seen them hold hands or kiss or show a sign of affection. The Jansons were similar to her parents. Even though Mrs. Janson was demanding, Mr. Janson looked at her lovingly. He would put his arm around her and squeeze her, and she would blush. River wondered if Mr. Janson knew about his wife's moods. *He must! She couldn't hide them from him, could she?*

Everyone said River and Joe's garland was wonderful, and so thoughtful. George had a huge smile when she watched it go up on the dining room wall. River was really glad she and Joe had made it. It'd been a way to avoid being with her best friend's mom, and it'd turned out to be something really special that she'd done for her best friend. There was a massive amount of food on the dining room table, like Thanksgiving and Christmas put together. Mrs. Janson had made a chocolate birthday cake with pink frosting and fancy decorations on it, like Cinderella's gown. It tasted amazing.

They gathered in the Jansons' family room to open presents. George's mom pointed out the latest renovations and what furniture was new. The adults weren't really paying attention to her, as they had been into happy hour for a couple of hours now, but they nodded at her as if they'd heard what she'd said. It was sort of sad.

Even though River's and Joe's moms were into art, they were the least snobby people you'd ever meet. *Still . . . was this part of Mrs. Janson's problem? Did she think they didn't like her? No, the moms get along. I've never heard them say anything bad about her. I have to stop trying to figure out what's wrong with George's mom. It's over my head.*

The party was over and Mrs. Janson was shooing everyone out. "River," her mom said. "Why don't you stay and help clean up? Mrs. Janson threw a fabulous party. It'd be nice if you'd stay and help." She kissed River's head and left before River could make up an excuse to not stay.

River walked into the kitchen. George looked surprised to see her. "You don't have to help clean up," said Mrs. Janson. She was tying a garbage bag full of paper party plates and cups and plastic silverware. She handed it to George.

"I'd like to," said River. George walked back into the kitchen. The two seemed calm, a sense of contentment filled the room.

"The table's cleared," Mrs. Janson said, "But I don't think we've collected all the wrapping paper and boxes."

George got another garbage bag, and she and River went into the family room. In here River felt a calmness too. She breathed a sigh of relief.

"Thank you for the birthday banner, again," said George. "Though I would've liked to have had you help me pick out the party things."

River's chest tightened. "Yes, I know." She wanted to ask George if it had gone smoothly.

The two filled the bag without talking.

"You can go now," said George. "Thanks." She didn't smile but she didn't look like she was hiding anything.

"Okay," said River. *It must have been uneventful at the Party Store.*

River walked home and saw the light on in her family's porch. Tomorrow morning she and her dad would be sitting there. Should she confess her concerns to him? Could she share enough with him before her mom and sister woke up? Keeping all her worries inside her wasn't making her stomach or her mind happy. Letting Joe know what had been happening hadn't made her feel relieved. She'd been surprised by that, but maybe sometimes, with very serious things that happened to her, she needed to tell at least one of her parents.

River was on the porch before her dad the next morning. She was looking at the pictures of Casper the Friendly Ghost in her comic book. She wished her dad would come in soon. Her mind had been too crowded with thoughts of the incidents with Mrs. Janson, and what she was going to say to her dad, to be able to stop and listen at the bedroom door before coming out. She wanted to get the discussion started!

"Good morning," her dad said. "You look bright-eyed this morning. And your hair is bushy-tailed." River couldn't help laughing at his silliness, which he showed sometimes.

She kept her mouth shut, letting him enjoy his coffee. *How many sips should I let him take before I start? One, two, three, four . . .*

"The sun's taking its time coming out this morning," Mr. Wren said.

River looked at the sky, which appeared to be on the other side of the lake. She hadn't been waiting for the sun to shine on the water like she did every other Sunday.

Her dad sighed and crossed his legs. "What are we going to talk about this morning?"

River jerked her head toward her dad. Why would he say that? He never had before. She said, "I don't feel comfortable with the way one of my friend's parents is acting."

"You don't?"

River wrapped her arms around her legs. The sun began showing itself on the water's surface. "It's Mrs. Janson," she said, and waited to see if he'd respond. He didn't. She went on. "There's something wrong with her." She wouldn't say more. She wanted his response to this.

He waited a moment, then said, "What do you think is wrong with George's mom?"

She watched her dad watch the scenery. "I don't know what is wrong with her."

"Has she done something?" He took a sip from her mom's beautiful ceramic mug. *I wish she'd stop making those stupid wall hangings and make her mugs again.*

River had decided that she'd begin with the event at the General Store. "Do you remember after the snowstorm, Mrs. Janson took me and George to the General Store to get George new boots?" And she told her dad the story. When she finished, he took a deep breath.

Was he going to be angry with her? Tell her she should respect adults no matter how they acted?

He looked at the entrance to the kitchen. "Let me fill my mug," he said. He returned, sat down, and placed his coffee on the table beside the chair. She couldn't tell if he didn't want to discuss the matter or if he was taking his time to figure out what to say to her.

They sat for a while not speaking. River watched the sun drag itself across the lake, up the hill, and onto their deck.

At this point, River was getting frustrated. It was getting close to the time her mom would be joining them. She wanted to hear from her dad. She wanted his opinion first. "Yeah?" She winced. Her voice came out sarcastic.

He sighed. "River, sometimes it's hard to understand why an adult acts a certain way." *No, not Dad! This is what other parents say to their kids! Not my dad.* "I'm sorry Mrs. Janson acted that way. I'm sure it was upsetting for you and George. But I don't know what to say to you. I—"

"Good morning," said River's mom. River closed her eyes. *Great.*

"Morning, Mom." River smiled and looked up at her.

"Feels like a serious conversation is going on in here!" Her mom stood at the window. She looked beautiful in her lime-green robe with the sun highlighting the red in her hair. River felt so thankful for having her mom.

"River and I were just going to check out the fish." Her dad got up with his mug in his hand and opened the door for her. They walked down to the dock. She stood beside him.

"Something *is* wrong with Mrs. Janson," her dad said. "I've never said anything to your mom or the dads or Mrs. Farrington."

She waited for him to say more, and when he didn't, she said, "Do you know what could be wrong with her?"

"I've no knowledge of that kind of stuff, River. I would have no clue." He crossed his arms while still holding his coffee mug. "I'm not happy you went through that experience with her at the General Store. Not one bit. And if I could say something to her, I would. If I could."

"I don't know how I can help George. I don't know what to do." The desperation in her voice surprised her.

"Just being there for her is probably all you can do." He sounded like he was done with their conversation, but River wasn't satisfied. She'd wanted more than a comforting talk. She wanted *some* answers!

"But Dad. I know how to be a good friend. I *am* being a good friend to George. I can't *not* be her friend, since the families are friends. I want to know *why* Mrs. Janson acts the way she does. I want to know *why* she gets so angry. I want her to fix herself so George doesn't have to live with a mother like her. So I don't have to be around someone like her when I just want to hang out with my best friend!"

"River, I'm a musician and a mechanic. What do you think I should know?" He looked at her, and he seemed as frustrated as she was.

"I just thought maybe you'd seen someone who acted like her before. That maybe Mr. Janson had said something to you." He turned and started walking toward the stairs. River followed.

"No. That's not something we would share." *Well, I hope I'm not like that when I grow up.*

"Doesn't anyone care about Mrs. Janson? Doesn't anyone want to help her? I don't think she wants to be the way she is." This morning with him had been a waste of time. A waste of a Sunday morning together. From now on, she wouldn't talk at all. She'd just sit with him. That would have to be enough.

At the top of the stairs her dad turned to her. "River, I'm sorry if I've let you down this morning, but I truly don't know what to say to you about George's mom. I agree that there is something in her brain that doesn't work right. We are friends with the Jansons and we always will be unless something unforeseen happens. But she's been this way since we've known her, and that's a long time."

"I'm going back down to the dock," she said. Her eyes stung, just like her heart. *They've known about her? For almost twenty years they've all known she needed help and no one helped her? How can adults be so cruel? I will never let George or Joe suffer like our parents allowed Mrs. Janson to suffer!* River held tight to the railing. She felt dizzy and sat on the wood step. The morning dew seemed to seep through her as she hung her head between her legs. This was all getting to be too much. She was too young to have to deal with this. This morning had turned into a complete disaster for her.

"River! River, breakfast is ready!" her mom yelled.

She joined them at the table and looked around at her family. They were passing platefuls of food; they were saying please and thank you. River had to calm down. She was in her own world, and no one was going to join her there. She had to relax and get back into theirs.

George and Joe both had docks (and beaches), but at some point the three had chosen the Wren dock as the one they hung out on. So, like many days before this one, they fished off it. After a time, they became fed up with the fish.

"Hey, look," said George. "Savannah's heading out the door. Should we follow her?"

"Yes!" River and Joe said.

They rested their fishing poles against the birch trees and started the trail. As they went past River's mom's studio, she came out. "Have you guys seen the Polaroid camera? I just realized I haven't seen it for a while. I need to take pictures of these wall hangings for a show. Can you keep an eye out for it?" They said they would.

Savannah was definitely going to the old barn today. And she was carrying the Polaroid! "Sneaky Savannah!" said River. They were far enough back that she was sure this time Savannah wasn't aware they were following her. They watched as she entered the barn. When they got to the entrance, the girls waited for Joe's directions.

"I'll go in first," he whispered. "Then you, River, and then you, George, follow behind. Let's try to be quiet and not let Savannah know we're here."

They followed Joe inside, watching their feet to make sure they weren't going to step on something that would creak. Joe stopped behind a beam, and River and George squatted down below him. They could see Savannah standing at the table that had had the leaves and wood on it the first time they followed her. All three of them gasped when Ralph walked in the door near the table and greeted Savannah.

Joe looked at his friends and they looked at him, with questioning gazes.

"What have you got today?" Ralph asked. He stood next to her and leaned over to look at what she had apparently placed on the table.

"I gathered pine needles and flowers. And—I found a tail! I think it's a squirrel's tail." River watched her sister examine the furry object, then place it on the table like she was a scientist. *Maybe she will be a scientist.*

"What have you been doing?" Savannah asked Ralph.

"I've been working with leaves. I gathered birch leaves and arranged them into circles so they almost look like suns." He pulled out Polaroid photos from his pocket and displayed them on the table.

"Oh! Those are nice!" She picked up one, then the next, and cooed at them all. "I'm going to work with rocks next. I'll make a picture I like, then take Polaroids of the art I made."

"I have to find out what they're doing," River whispered. The other two nodded.

"What are you guys doing?" She stopped at the table. "These photos are cool, Ralph."

The other two came up behind her. She handed one of the photos to Joe. He nodded. "I've seen something like this in one of my mom's art magazines. You two have been making Earth art?"

"Hi, guys!" Ralph smiled. "Yes. You've caught us making art. That's all. Nothing mysterious. Savannah told me you were spying on us. So we decided the Three Detectives Club should discover what we were up to instead of us telling you." He looked at River, then George. "Joe told me about your detectives club."

"I said I'd ask you two if Ralph could join," explained Joe.

"Sure," said River. "But what are you making here?"

"I'm making art, like Joe said," said Ralph. "I'm using things I find in nature. Leaves, twigs, acorns. And your sister is my assistant."

River picked up a dried purple flower. "Looks fun!"

"Savannah saw me making one of my pieces in the woods one day, and stopped and asked what I was doing. Then she asked if she could be my assistant, and I said she could if her parents said it was okay. But it looks like she didn't ask her parents," Ralph explained. "Anyway, I arrange things on the ground and take a photo of them." He pointed to the camera on the corner of the table.

"And you're helping him, Savannah? Are you sure Ralph wants your help?"

"Yes," Savannah said. Ralph nodded. "And since I'm his apprentice, I'm learning how to make Earth art too." Her eyes shined with excitement. River smiled at her. Then she frowned.

"Savannah, why did you take Mom's Polaroid if Ralph has a camera?"

"Because I wanted to take pictures of my work too. Ralph's camera is too good for me to use."

"Someday I'll let you use it," said Ralph. Savannah shrieked with delight.

"This *is* impressive, Ralph!" said Joe. "I'd like to see the photographs you've taken of your other pieces. Maybe my mom will have an exhibit of your art someday."

"Well," said Ralph, blushing, "maybe someday after I've been doing this for a while."

"After he takes pictures of what he's made," Savannah said, "then he leaves the materials and nature messes them up! It's so amazing. Wait till you see what he made with icicles and snow! He was going to make gigantic snowballs, but the snow melted before he could make them big enough."

"We should return Mom's camera," said River. "Once we tell Mom and Dad all about your new career, maybe they will get you your own camera." Savannah cheered.

The three detectives walked back home, leaving Ralph and Savannah to make their art. They decided to go to River's house and discuss their next case.

"We've solved our first case!" said George.

As they walked, Joe looked at the two members of his detective club. "That was a pretty easy case to solve for our first one."

"So my sister *is* making art. I wouldn't have guessed that," said River.

"I think I may have our second case," said George. She stopped in her tracks and took a letter out of her coat pocket.

"Really?" Joe's eyebrows raised. "What is it?" River also wondered what it would be.

"It's a letter," George said. "It was in my mom's *Diet for a Small Planet* cookbook. After reading it, I felt mad at Truance because she left me to live with our mom without the support of my sister. It's been like seven years that my sister's been gone. We don't know where she is."

She read:

> January 6, 1971
>
> Dear Mom,
>
> I won't let you treat me this way anymore. I'm tired of the mean things you've said to me. You'll probably say I'm being sensitive and that you didn't mean what you said or that I misunderstood what you said to me. So, let me remind you of some of your comments: "You'll never find anyone. You'll be alone." "You get what you want." "You don't appreciate how hard your dad and I work to give you and your sister what you have. You're a spoiled princess."

> These are a few of the gems you said to me. For a long time I believed that I was what you told me I was. A selfish brat. I thought I wasn't worthy of having good things happen to me. So, even though I will miss Dad and George terribly, I'm leaving. Because I woke up one day and for some reason realized that I am a good person and do deserve good things happening to me. And most importantly, I don't deserve being told by you that I am not deserving of happiness.
>
> Truance

"How did you know that was our other case?" asked Joe. River was glad she and Joe had decided to keep their case about Mrs. Janson to themselves.

"One time when we were studying at your house, you left your case notes in your bedroom."

"Oh," said Joe. "Sorry we didn't ask you first if we could try to find your sister."

George shook her head. "It's okay. I really wish she was around with my mom acting so . . ."

"What do you want us to do?" asked Joe, even though River knew he was hankering to get the missing person investigation going.

"I want to find her."

"Your mom and dad haven't heard from her at all?" said River. "Where would we start?"

"I remember your parents went to the police," Joe said, putting his hand to his chin. "But that's all I remember."

"We were maybe six years old?" added River.

"Yes," answered George. "The police didn't get anywhere. They tried for as long as they were supposed to, then gave up. I don't know how we could ever find her." She shrugged. "Like finding out what's wrong with my mom. This is probably impossible."

"'Many things are possible just as long as you don't know they're impossible,'" answered Joe. When they stared at him he said, "It's from *The Phantom Tollbooth*. One of my all-time favorite books."

After school on the first day back from spring break, the three went to the library to ask the librarian how they should start looking for George's sister. "Microfiche," said the librarian. River knew that microfiche was a type of film that could hold more than one hundred pages of print newspapers. They were set up at the microfiche machine, and Joe began going through the local newspapers from 1971 through 1973. George and River sat in chairs on either side of him. They found an article about Truance going missing, then a month later an update on the case, then two months later an article saying the Jansons hoped their daughter would return to them, and that they missed her terribly and only wanted to know she was safe.

"Should we go through more newspapers?" asked Joe. The other two nodded.

For another hour and a half they whirled through pages and pages of regional and national newspapers, but found nothing.

When they were tired and River's stomach was calling for food, she suggested, "Maybe we should talk to Beth. They were friends, weren't they?"

"Yes," said Joe and George together.

"I think that's our next step. We should stop for today and get something to eat." Joe signaled to the librarian that they were done. River and George snickered. "It's like he works here already and he's their boss!" George whispered to River. "Let's make sandwiches and go down to the dock."

They dangled their feet in the lake water as they sat on River's dock eating sandwiches.

"I feel better," said George, interrupting the silence that had been between them. River had been listening to the waves and the speedboats. She and Joe told her they were glad.

"We'll talk to Beth tomorrow," said Joe.

"I've got to help my dad with one of his renovations; Mom will be shopping for new furniture. So you'll let me know what Beth says."

River and George sat at Joe's family's kitchen table waiting for his parents to finish the weekly updates on everyone's lives. Joe wouldn't have to take the telephone receiver into his bedroom. Beth had called in the early evening on a Saturday, not on her regular Sunday. Saturday evening was happy hour for the parents. So the two detectives were getting a break from having to come up with an excuse for talking to Beth. After talking with their daughter, the Farringtons would be joining the Wrens for a happy-hour cruise around the lake. The Jansons weren't coming this time because, as George had said, they were working on the house.

River and Joe sat at the table and put the earpiece between them. Joe said, "We were wondering if you know anything about Truance leaving."

"Oh," said Beth, in a surprised voice. "I haven't heard her name mentioned in a long time. Why are you asking?"

River spoke. "George found a letter that Truance wrote to their mom. She may have written it on the day she left."

Joe continued. "River and George and I want to see if we can find Truance. We went to the library and went through microfiche from local newspapers from 1971 through 1973, and found only the article about Truance leaving, and updates on the search. Our next step is finding out if you remember anything about Truance wanting to leave or if she said anything to you."

"Let me think about it," was Beth's response. River noted reserve or reluctance in Beth's voice. *Were Beth and Truance not really friends?*

Sunday arrived. Again, no George (and no reason as to why). River and Joe sat in the same kitchen chairs waiting for his parents to sign off. As before, there was the handoff of the phone from his parents to him, followed by Joe and River trotting off to his bedroom.

Beth began talking first. "I've thought about the time around when Truance left home. And I'm sorry, but I don't remember much." River sighed. Scratchy jumped onto the bed. River held out her hand and he came up to her so she could rub his head.

Joe asked, "What do you remember?"

"Truance and I weren't that close. We were friends, but she had kind of distanced herself from me. I didn't see her that much right before she left."

"Did Truance talk about places she'd like to go or see?" asked River.

"She—she did say she'd seen an article about small towns in New York and how that state was very pretty. Kind of like New Jersey—people who haven't been here think it's just the turnpike; similar to how people often think New York is only the city, not all the lakes and scenery. And Connecticut, she wanted to visit there too. I remember there was a boy who'd moved here from Connecticut who she had a crush on."

"That might be something," said Joe.

"I'm sorry, guys. I've really thought about this all week. Even looked through our yearbooks. I can't think of where Truance would have gone or why she left in the first place."

Coming back into the bedroom after hanging up the phone, Joe said, "We might have something. New York and Connecticut, or here in New Jersey."

"Right," said River. "But I think we're at a dead end. We're kids. We've done all we can. We cared at least to try to find answers." She shrugged. "I know, it's frustrating."

Joe shrugged too. "Yeah, but you're right. We have to stick to things like tracking little sisters right now."

JULY

It was late afternoon in Rocky Hill. School had ended; summer had begun. The Three Detectives Club was still open for business, but a case hadn't presented itself yet. Savannah and Ralph continued creating their Earth art, and Mrs. Wren had cleared a space in her studio for them to work. Mrs. Farrington was putting up an exhibit of landscape watercolor paintings by local artists. River, George, and Joe were assisting her. Joe's job was to hold the framed paintings on the wall. River made sure the pieces were straight by using a level, then she hammered in the nail, and Joe hung the piece. George came next with a label and adhesive to attach on the right side.

Mrs. Farrington came over and nodded at their work. She turned to River. "Have you reminded your mom that I'm planning an exhibit of New Jersey ceramic artists in the fall?"

"Yes, I did. It seems like she's becoming interested. I think my mom's getting tired of making smiley faces and lambs."

George snickered. "I imagine she would be. I don't know much about art, but I think your mom's mugs and bowls are really good."

"They are," agreed Joe's mom. "If only she could find the confidence she needs to get back to making them." She walked over to a window. River heard her gasp and looked to see her move closer to the glass. "Is that . . . ? Could it be her?"

"Is someone outside the gallery?" asked Joe, seeing his mom's perplexed expression.

"There's a car parked across the street, which is strange. Usually people park in front of my gallery, not across the road," stated Mrs. Farrington. "And there's a young woman walking toward the building."

George put down the label and walked over to the window. River followed, her heart pounding.

A young woman with long blonde hair wearing a plaid jumper was approaching the gallery door. George sucked in air. “George?” asked River. “Is it . . . is that Truance?” River had seen photos of Truance, but only vaguely remembered what she looked like. It turned out she looked just like George.

“It is Truance,” said Mrs. Farrington, smiling and opening the door. “Truance! What a wonderful surprise!” She stepped aside so George’s sister could enter.

“Hi, Mrs. Farrington! I hoped your gallery was still here. I’m such an art lover. There’s this wonderful art museum in Ridgefield, Connecticut, called the Aldrich Contemporary Art . . .”

George stepped behind River. River almost laughed. Her friend was acting like a shy child.

“George,” said Truance, tilting her head so she could see her sister. “Hi, George. It’s so great to see you.” She stayed still, but River saw a slight anxious twitch in her figure.

“Hi, Truance,” said George, stepping out from behind River. “Hi,” she said again, and hugged her. The sisters seemed to melt into each other. “I’m so, so glad you’re back!”

Truance told them she was staying at a friend's place nearby. She wasn't sure of her plans, but she wanted to reconnect with her family. "If it works out, maybe I'll move back? It's a great area."

George left with her sister. River couldn't remember how long it'd been since she'd seen her friend look so happy.

That night in bed, River stared at the ceiling. She wished she could be a fly on the wall when Truance had walked into her house with George—Truance's car had been parked at the Jansons' house all evening. She hoped George would tell her everything about their mom's recent behavior. *How will this change things in their family? Will it make things better or not?* River sighed. She had her family—and her heritage that she wanted to continue learning about. And maybe one day her dad would be interested in learning about the Lenni-Lenape too.

She moved her legs and felt High-Five at the end of her bed. She kept thinking: about her dad, the other adults, and Mrs. Janson instead. Her dad had told her that they'd known about Mrs. Janson's odd behavior. Had he called it odd? She couldn't remember. How could they think that this was okay? Was normal? She clutched the sheets. *The adults just ignored George's mom's behavior. . . . Would I have done the same?* Had they witnessed the same behavior as she and George had? If they had, how could they not want to do something about it? Why hadn't they wanted to help their friend? *I would never let George or Joe suffer like they've let Mrs. Janson suffer.* Tears ran down her cheeks.

River was angry when she sat down to breakfast the next morning. Her mom even commented that she looked mad. River ignored her questioning as to why.

Her dad was filling his mug with coffee. "Savannah, slow down. You're going to choke on your cereal," he told her. He looked at River. "What's wrong with you this morning?"

She looked at the empty ceramic bowl in front of her. "You taught Savannah and I to be good friends." Her dad nodded. Her mom walked over and put a hand on River's shoulder. "Aren't you supposed to help a friend if she's having trouble with someone?"

"Is George going through something?" her mom asked. "Have you talked to her since Truance returned?" River shook her head.

She couldn't keep what was bothering her inside anymore. "I'm worried about George because her mom sometimes overreacts. She gets really happy and then really upset, and you don't know what she's going to do." Her parents' expressions hadn't changed. Her cheeks warmed again. "You knew she acted this way!" she yelled at them. Her dad leaned against the counter; her mom took her hand away from River's shoulder.

"You knew she acted this way!" River repeated. "You knew for years that she—she could've been in mental pain. Suffering! Do you think she likes acting like she does? Because from what I've experienced, I don't think she does! Don't you *care* about your friend?"

Savannah stared at River with watery eyes. "Sorry, Savannah," said River.

Her mom spoke first. "Dear, it's not easy. You have to decide how involved you want to become. What you think is appropriate."

"Appropriate?" River asked. "Like whether to accept an invitation to a tea party? The last couple of months I've been trying to figure out how to help George. We tried to find out what is wrong with her mom. We couldn't. There's nothing we could do—"

"See?" said her mom.

"There's nothing we could do," River repeated, "because we are only *kids*. But *you* are adults and *you* should have done something to help your friend who is suffering." She stood up and walked out the door. She didn't want to hear their excuses. She wanted to see how George was. She'd hear from her dad later how unacceptable her behavior had been.

George's face glowed like the sun when she opened the door and greeted River. Truance and their mom were sitting on the couch in the family room (the latest renovation was a new door where a window had been). Their dad wasn't there. River's eyes went to Mrs. Janson's shiny cheeks. A pile of tissues in front of her indicated to River that Mrs. Janson was having complicated emotions that morning.

"Hi, River," said Truance. Expertly applied makeup on her pretty face appeared to be untouched by any emotions. "How are you?" River replied that she was fine.

"We're listening to what Truance has been doing," said George. "She may work for Mrs. Farrington!"

When Mrs. Janson smiled at River, her beautiful face showed wrinkles that River hadn't noticed before.

"Truance has done a lot since she left," George continued. "She's taken college classes and may apply to Princeton! She also talked with Joe's mom about majoring in art history. Let's go in my room." River followed her into the room, then sat on a beanbag on the shag carpet. She dragged her fingers through the carpet. "Where's your dad?" she asked.

"Dad's working on cabinets. He left early this morning. Said he'd be late. He's not so happy to have Truance back, I think."

"And your mom? How's she?" River asked.

"Seems okay. Hasn't had a fit, yet." George plopped onto the beanbag next to River.

"You know all the parents knew your mom had problems and no one tried to help her," River said. She'd had it with keeping any information from those that it concerned.

"And what am I supposed to say to that? How is that supposed to make me feel, River?"

This was more like George. *Let her get mad. Like I am.* "Her friends let your mom suffer. Your sister left, and you and your dad had to live with your mom, with no one caring about how that would affect you and him. And now Truance decides she can come back. How does that make you feel?"

"I *feel* that it's none of your business. I think you should keep your nose out of other families' problems! Why are you so interested in my family? Is your family too boring for you? I suggest you leave us alone!" She stood up. "You should go."

River went. But she thought of an idea on the way home. To answer George's question, she didn't know why she cared about Mrs. Janson's well-being when no one else did. Maybe that was just how she was. She said out loud, "Anyway, a week from today is the Fourth of July, and I have an idea!"

On the Fourth of July, Joe, George, and River had their assignments. It wasn't a mystery case they'd taken on. It was a case that would maybe help Mrs. Janson feel better, at least on her birthday. And for her to know that her friends and their kids were there for her and loved her.

First, River needed to speak with her dad. "This is a surprise," he said, poking his head up from an engine as she walked into his shop. "I can't remember, are you still grounded for speaking to your mom and me the way you did?"

"I am no longer grounded. And for the record, I did apologize. I have a request."

"Yes?" He wiped his hands with a greasy towel. She loved the smell of grease; she'd smelled it all her life.

"George, Joe, and I are planning a special birthday for Mrs. Janson. You do remember it's her birthday on the Fourth of July?"

"Yes. I do remember."

"As you know, she loves her Mustang. So I would like you to offer her a year of free care for it."

"Is that so? And I am supposed to just forget about the money that I will lose?"

River stood tall. She'd prepared for this. "This is the least you owe Mrs. Janson, for not being a good friend all these years." River held up her hand to her dad's protest. "I don't care if you ground me again. You were not a good friend. One year free maintenance." She held out her hand. Shaking it, he said, "My daughter, the kindest person I know."

Her visit to her mom's studio was much easier, because Joe had presented their idea to his mom and Mrs. Farrington had presented her own idea to River's mom.

Her mom explained to her, "Mrs. Farrington has agreed to ask Mrs. Janson to cater the next gallery opening. She said that the problem had been that Mrs. Janson didn't have enough pie pans to bake the small pies. So"—her mom held up a miniature pie pan, which would hold a two-bite pie—"what do you think?"

"It's so cute. But how many do you have to make?"

"I will make a dozen. And then I can keep making them—and I made smaller ones that can be pendants." Her mom picked up a pendant-size ceramic circle. "See?"

"Yes!" River's chest warmed. So far, the parents seemed to be into her idea.

"And," her mom continued, "I made one for you." She handed River one of the pendants. This one had a turtle on it.

"A turtle. You mean, like from the Lenape creation story? How did you know?"

Her mom kissed the top of River's head. "We need to learn about the Lenni-Lenape heritage."

Later that night the sound of fireworks rang out across Lake Saturday, and kids were running around with sparklers. And the three families sat around the Wrens' bonfire. They had finished eating dinner and birthday cake, and now the kids had gathered in front of George's mom. Behind them was a large tarp.

Mrs. Janson had her hair in swooping curls. Instead of a fancy outfit she wore a plaid shirt, blue jeans, and navy sneakers. She looked comfortable, just one of the moms.

"Mom," George said, "now it's time for your presents. Mr. Wren?"

River's dad stood and walked over to George's mom with a paper in his hand. "Here's a certificate that Joe made that states Wren's Garage is offering you one year of free service for your Mustang."

"Oh, how nice!" Mrs. Janson said, nodding at him. "Thank you!"

River and Joe stepped forward and said, "Our moms each have something for you."

"Mom," said River.

Mrs. Wren stood up, holding a dish towel covering a saucer-shaped object. Pulling away the towel, she said, "I made this ceramic pie dish for you." Then she laughed. "I was using this shape for my smiley face and lamb wall hangings, but I think it's much better as a pie dish."

"I love periwinkle blue," Mrs. Janson said, "and the golden-brown glaze. Thank you." Her smile was beautiful.

Next, Mrs. Farrington stood. "I'd love to have your pies at my gallery openings, if you would be interested."

Mrs. Janson hugged her neighbor and friend. "Oh, thank you. I would love to."

The moms hugged, laughed, then wiped away tears.

Once they'd returned to their seats, George, with an awkward grin, took her mom's hand and turned to Beowulf's Brother. Joe removed the tarp to reveal the band's instruments.

Mr. Janson said to his wife, "I wrote you a song about how important you are to me."

"The first song you've written for me. See how wonderful your dad is?" She squeezed George's hand.

Mr. Wren added, "Beowulf's Brother's first love song."

They played the heavy metal acoustic song, and the music traveled across and up and down the lake. When the tune ended with River's dad playing the last note, the group clapped and hollered and agreed it was Beowulf's Brother's best song yet. The cheers they heard from around the lake confirmed it. After that it got sort of hokey, with everyone hugging and saying they loved each other.

That night River was tucked into her bed when her dad came in and hugged her. He hadn't embraced any of the adults or kids at the bonfire. It wasn't his style. The room was dark and quiet except for the night-light and the sound of Savannah snoring in the bed next to her. Her chest filled with happiness for what George, Joe, and she had done for George's mom. River didn't expect the night's events to change Mrs. Janson's life or life in the Janson household. Maybe she'd planned the evening as a way to make herself feel good. She hoped not—or maybe that was okay. Either way, it was the only thing River had been able to think of to help ease George's difficult circumstance.

The next Sunday came and River was up first. The door creaked as she opened it. *I always forget about the door!* On the deck, the metal chair also squeaked as she sat in it. But a pleasing sound graced her ears, a bird's call. *Is that a mockingbird? . . . There it is again.* River sighed with a smile. The sun was coming up through the trees and making its way across the water to her side of the lake.

The tranquility would only be interrupted by the sounds of motorboats, chain saws, and cars, the signals of people getting their day started. She sat for a while listening to the bird that she'd decided was a mockingbird.

"You won." Again the door creaked, then it clicked as her dad came out. She watched him situate himself in the chair beside her, his cup of steaming coffee in one hand and the newspaper in the other. "It came early," he said, waggling the paper. He set the coffee on the deck and scanned the front page.

River wasn't sure if she liked the newspaper interfering with their time together. She heard the bird speak once more before it flew away, as if allowing River and her dad to talk. Minutes went by . . . her dad continued to look through the paper. River ran her hand along the hem of her nightgown.

"Hmm," he said, breaking the silence, "isn't this interesting?" Her dad's tone signaled he was implying the opposite. "Seems like they're going to teach you about the Nanticoke Lenni-Lenape culture in school now."

River let go of her nightgown and sat up. She had information to add to this. "I heard the librarian say the tribe changed their official name to 'Nanticoke Lenni-Lenape Indians of New Jersey.'"

"Oh. Did they?" he responded.

"Yes." Before he could change the subject, which she suspected he would, she said, "You know that book we have on the shelf, *Delaware's Forgotten Folk*? I'm reading it. The illustrations from the book were in the exhibit at Mrs. Farrington's gallery, remember? It has interesting things about our heritage. You've read the book, right, Dad?"

"Maybe. I don't remember." He'd put down the paper to sip his coffee.

Undaunted, she continued. "There's so much of our people's history that I'm learning about, so I guess I'll be ahead of the game when they start teaching it to us." She imagined sitting in school feeling proud as her classmates learned about her people.

Her dad crossed his arms. "Your uncle's and my teachers didn't seem interested in the topic. Only one that I can remember talked about the local tribes."

"Who was the teacher?" Her heart pounded faster. He'd never spoken to her about his experience in school.

His eyes staring forward, he began, "His name was Mr. McCarthy. His hobby was archaeology. He wanted to create a village like those built by the Lenni-Lenape Indians. He was a very excitable man, I remember. He would tell us, 'I want to expand on what is taught in your textbook! I want you to experience what it was like to be one of the original people of this area!' . . . and then his hand would sweep over to me, the only Indian in the classroom, and say, 'Like Robert Wren, here.' I didn't like it when he did that, singled me out. I felt embarrassed and even more different from my classmates. If he thought it would make me feel special or proud of who I was, it didn't. Instead, I was ashamed."

"*Ashamed?* Why would you feel ashamed, Dad?"

"Because I felt a painful sense of having done something wrong. That our people had done something wrong."

Her heart beat faster as she realized this was the first time in her life she'd heard her dad say "our people" when speaking about the Lenape tribe.

"I don't understand," she said.

At that moment, another mockingbird chirped above her.

Her dad said, "I remember thinking, why would these white male historians talk about how their people destroyed our land and our culture, and at the same time come across as proud about what they'd done to us? Even if my history teachers didn't mean to—and I generally don't think they did—they were teaching me and the few others who were from the Lenape tribes that we had done something wrong. *We* should be ashamed of ourselves because we didn't stand up to the white man. We didn't force them to leave. It was our fault. And every American history book said so. No triumphs were recorded, only what we hadn't accomplished." She saw his facial muscles tighten.

In *Forgotten Folk,* River had read facts like the Lenape Indians lived in round houses called wigwams or larger dwellings called longhouses, but she understood that this wasn't the point her dad was making.

Suddenly the tense muscles on his face relaxed. "But now . . . you might actually *learn* more about the tribe. Maybe they'll get some things *right* this time." He picked up the newspaper and found the article. "'The purpose of the revised curriculum is to eliminate stereotypes of Native Americans and to increase public awareness of the tribes.' We'll see."

"It's a start," said River. The mockingbird replied in agreement.

He looked at her and smiled. "By the way, that book you're talking about. I used to take it off your grandparents' shelf and read it, when I was your age."

"You did?" Her heart expanded with joy.

"Mr. McCarthy did eventually establish a replica Lenape village."

"I know! My class has been there. I liked it." *I wonder how authentic it is.*

"It's not from the Lenape perspective," he told her, "but it's better than nothing."

A thought sprang into River's mind. "Dad, I have an idea: you could volunteer there! We must have relatives around here. And there's a tribal commission or something like that here, isn't there?"

"I could." Then he added, "You always have ideas for me, River."

She laughed. "But you should, Dad! Then you could teach me and Savannah! And talk to our classes!"

"Whoa, cowgirl, hold your horses. I haven't even said I like the suggestion."

"Well!" River turned to see her mom standing beside her. "I've been watching you two from the window. You seem to be discussing something important."

River smiled at her mom and shrugged. Her mom hadn't heard her and her dad's discussion. And she was glad, content that their talk had remained between them. Her dad may have felt the same way, because he stood up and said he should start the eggs. As he passed her he put his hand on her shoulder and squeezed. He rarely showed his affection that way.

River looked up at the tree and spotted the mockingbird. She nodded at it, and it sang a few more notes. She could have sworn it returned her nod before it flew away.

ACKNOWLEDGMENTS

I would like to thank my family and friends for their boundless love and support.

And a special thank-you to all of my Women Writing for Change ladies. Thank you for the joy you bring: Gina, Mel, Ganit, Melody, Lorena, and Karen.

GLOSSARY

Andy Goldsworthy (1956–): a contemporary/ Earth artist who creates site-specific artwork in natural and urban settings using materials from nature.

Art: objects created for purely aesthetic reasons by human beings to evoke emotions, feelings, and thoughts in the viewer.

Art history: a subject anyone can be interested in that relates to how we see art, how we interpret art, what art means to us, and how it makes us feel. It is also the study of how art was made around the world, who made it, and when. When studying the history of art, ask: When in history was it made? Where was it made? By whom (a person or group of people)? Why was it made, for what purpose?

Artist: a person who creates art objects, ideas, or concepts as a career or a hobby.

Artwork: an artistic production that involves skill and knowledge of using natural and manufactured materials that are combined with imagination and creativity to make an original object or concept.

Bisque: a piece of pottery that has been fired but not glazed.

Casting: a way to make a piece of pottery by placing the clay into a mold.

Ceramics: from Greek, meaning "earthen vessel," which refers to a range of types of objects such as pottery, china, tiles, and bricks.

Christo (1935–2020): contemporary/Earth artist who wrapped gigantic areas of land and water with brightly colored plastic.

Clay: a fine-grained natural material; the oldest known art material, dating back to prehistoric humans, who used it for making pottery.

Color: how light is refracted onto an object. Color has three attributes: hue or tint—the actual color; intensity—degree of purity or strength; value—the lightness or darkness. Red, orange, yellow, green, blue, and violet are created by light.

Complementary colors: the result of mixing two primary colors.

Composition: the way elements are arranged in a picture; also applies to writing and music.

Crafts: a hobby or an occupation that requires a particular skill and knowledge of a specific medium or media (plural).

Craftsperson: an artist who makes crafts that usually have a functional purpose.

Decorative arts: objects made for practical uses, such as a ceramic mug or bowl.

Dipping: applying glaze to pottery by dipping it into a container of glaze, then letting the excess drain off.

Earth art: art made with nature and in natural landscapes. It is often photographed because of its impermanence.

Environmental art: similar to Earth art, in that it is mainly made of natural materials, but may vary because of an ecological and/or political theme.

Fine art: art made for viewing and interpreting rather than functional purposes.

Firing: a process for baking clay at a high temperature in order to harden it.

Glaze: a permanent (through firing), glass-like coating put on the surface of a piece of pottery. It adds color and decoration to a piece.

Jeanne-Claude (1935–2009): a contemporary/Earth artist noted for her large-scale artwork; she often collaborated on art projects with Christo.

Kiln: oven used to fire clay pieces.

Medium or media (plural): material such as oil and acrylic paint, marble, metal, wood, video, or a combination of materials, called mixed media, that is used to make an artwork.

Potter's wheel: a machine with a motorized turntable used to shape clay into a form.

Pottery: a process to make objects with clay, which when fired give them a durable form.

Relief: an artwork that projects from its surface in three dimensions.

Sculpture: a three-dimensional work of art made of various materials, such as bronze or wood.

Robert Smithson (1938–1973): an Earth artist whose best-known work is *Spiral Jetty* (1970), a 1,500-foot-long, 15-foot-wide spiral form constructed from local basalt rocks in Utah.

Sketch: marks made on paper with a pencil or pen or other held instrument; a drawing, painting, or model made as a rough draft for the final work of art.

Throwing: a technique of forming pottery by placing a ball of clay on a potter's wheel, then, as the motorized wheel turns, shaping it with one's hands.

Tint: a color made by adding white to make it lighter (see Color).

Visual arts: forms of art, such as painting, sculpture, photography, and drawing.

RESOURCES

WEBSITES

1970s: What was happening? https://www.history.com/topics/1970s/1970s

http://www.thepeoplehistory.com/1970s.html

Delaware Nanticoke Lenape Tribe: https://www.pinterest.com/bobbihow/delaware-nanticoke-lenape-tribe/

Facts for Now: https://factsfornow.scholastic.com/book?uid=10765735&id=10020743&searchTerm=New+Jersey&iter=0

The Lenape Center: https://thelenapecenter.com

Lenape Nation of Pennsylvania: https://www.lenape-nation.org

The Nanticoke Lenni-Lenape: An American Indian Tribe: https://nanticoke-lenape.info/community.htm

New Jersey Almanac—Native Americans: https://www.newjerseyalmanac.com/native-americans.html
Princeton Magazine: http://www.princetonmagazine.com
Princeton Township: https://www.princetonnj.gov
Princeton University: https://www.princeton.edu
Rocky Hill: http://www.rockyhill-nj.gov
Sourland Mountain Preserve: http://www.somersetcountyparks.org/parksfacilities/sourland/sourlandmtpreserve.html

BOOKS

American Girl series, Julie (1974–1977) by Megan McDonald
American Girl series, Kaya (1764–1766) by Janet Shaw
Ancestor Approved: Intertribal Stories for Kids edited by Cynthia Leitich Smith (2021)
Andy's Snowball Story by Kristin McGlothlin (2009)
Apple in the Middle by Dawn Quigley (2020)

Archie by Bill Golliher, illustrated by Pat and Tim Kennedy (1939–present)

ArtSpeak: A Guide to Contemporary Ideas, Movements, and Buzzwords, 1945 to the Present by Robert Atkins (2013)

Beowulf, translation by David Wright (1957)

Beowulf, translation by Maria Dahvana Headley (2020)

Casper the Friendly Ghost by cocreators Seymour Victory Reit and Joseph Oriolo (1939–2012)

The Country of the Pointed Firs by Sarah Orne Jewett, foreword by Willa Cather (2001)

Delaware: Lenape by Joseph Stanley (2016)

Enclosure by Andy Goldsworthy (2007)

Encyclopedia Brown series (1963–2012) by Donald J. Sobol, illustrated by Leonard Shortall

Fry Bread by Kevin Noble Maillard, illustrated by Juana Martinez-Neal (2019)

The Guerrilla Girls' Bedside Companion to the History of Western Art by Guerrilla Girls (1998)

The Hardy Boys Stories by Franklin W. Dixon (1927–present)

The Honest Art Dictionary: A Jovial Trip through Art Jargon by Natalie De La Torre, Corrie Hendricks, Jennifer Gutierrez, and Virginia Van Dine (2020)

I Can Make This Promise by Christine Day (2019)

Island of the Blue Dolphins by Scott O'Dell (1960)

Just Looking: Essays on Art by John Updike (1989)

Landscapes for Art: Contemporary Sculpture Parks edited by Glenn Harper and Twylene Moyer (2008)

Me and My Feelings: A Kids' Guide to Understanding and Expressing Themselves by Vanessa Green Allen, M.Ed., NBCT (2019)

Meeting Miss 405 by Lois Peterson (2008)

Midsummer Snowballs by Andy Goldsworthy (2001)

Modern Art: A Crash Course by Cory Bell (2001)

My Ántonia by Willa Cather (1918)

The Nancy Drew Mystery Stories by Carolyn Keene

The Clue of the Black Keys, ghostwriters Wilhelmina Rankin and Harriet Stratemeyer Adams (1951)

The Hidden Window Mystery, ghostwriter Harriet Stratemeyer Adams (1956)

The Phantom of Pine Hill, ghostwriter Harriet Stratemeyer Adams (1965)

The New Earthwork: Art, Action, Agency edited by Twylene Moyer and Glenn Harper (2012)

New Jersey by Deborah Kent (1987)

New Jersey: The Garden State by John Hamilton (1992)

The Nine-Ton Cat: Behind the Scenes at an Art Museum by Peggy Thomson with Barbara Moore, edited by Carol Eron (1997)

O Pioneers! by Willa Cather (1913)

The People of Twelve Thousand Winters by Trinka Hakes Noble (2011)

The Phantom Tollbooth by Norton Juster, illustrated by Jules Feiffer (1961)

Pocahontas Leads the Way by Tessa Roehl, illustrated by Rosa La Barbera (2020)

Rainbow Crow: A Lenape Tale by Nancy Van Laan (1991)

Sarah Orne Jewett: An American Persephone by Sarah Way Sherman (1989)

The Sea in Winter by Christine Day (2021)

Sisters of the Neversea by Cynthia Leitich Smith (2021)

The Three Investigators series by Robert Arthur (1964–1987)

The Troll Garden by Willa Cather (1961)

Two-Minute Mysteries (1969–1975) by Donald J. Sobol

We Are Grateful: Otsaliheliga by Traci Sorell, illustrated by Frané Lessac (2018)

We Are Still Here!: Native American Truths Everyone Should Know by Traci Sorell (2021)

We Are Still Here!: The Tribal Saga of New Jersey's Nanticoke and Lenape Indians by John R. Norwood (2007)

Why a Painting Is Like a Pizza: A Guide to Understanding and Enjoying Modern Art by Nancy G. Heller (2002)

ABOUT THE AUTHOR

© Ron White

Before creating the Sourland Mountain series, Kristin McGlothlin was the assistant curator of education at the Norton Museum of Art, where she designed and managed the Norton's art and music programs. She has a BA in art history and a BA and MA in English. The first book in the Sourland Mountain series, *Drawing with Whitman,* won the 2019 Moonbeam Children's Book Awards

Silver Medal for Pre-Teen Fiction and received an honorable mention in the 2020 Readers' Favorite International Book Awards for children grades four through six. The second book in the series, *Listen,* won the 2021 Moonbeam Children's Book Awards Silver Medal for Pre-Teen Fiction. A writer since she was thirteen, now, like a million years later, Kristin has settled upon writing as her career. She lives in Jupiter, Florida.

CPSIA information can be obtained
at www.ICGtesting.com
Printed in the USA
BVHW071942220222
629775BV00001B/205

9 781733 286527